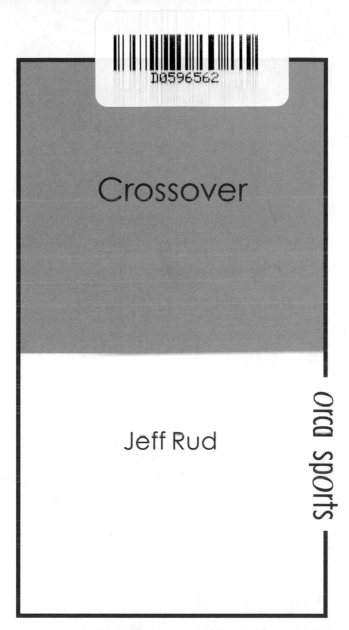

Crossover

Jeff Rud

orca sports

Orca Book Publishers

Library and Archives Canada Cataloguing in Publication

Rud, Jeff, 1960-
Crossover / written by Jeff Rud.

(Orca sports)
ISBN 978-1-55143-981-5

I. Title. II. Series.

PS8635.U32C76 2008   jC813'.6   C2008-900187-7

Summary: Kyle is a rising basketball star, but his interest in theater
causes huge problems both on and off the court.

First published in the United States, 2008
Library of Congress Control Number: 2008920114

Orca Book Publishers gratefully acknowledges the support for its publishing
programs provided by the following agencies: the Government of Canada
through the Book Publishing Industry Development Program and the
Canada Council for the Arts, and the Province of British Columbia through
the BC Arts Council and the Book Publishing Tax Credit.

Cover design by Teresa Bubela
Cover photography by Getty Images

Orca Book Publishers
PO Box 5626, Stn. B
Victoria, BC Canada
V8R 6S4

Orca Book Publishers
PO Box 468
Custer, WA USA
98240-0468

www.orcabook.com
Printed and bound in Canada.

11 10 09 08 • 4 3 2 1

For my dearest Maggie,
who inspired this story.

Acknowledgments

I would like to thank Orca publisher, Bob Tyrrell, and associate publisher, Andrew Wooldridge, for their continued support, as well as editor Sarah Harvey for her patience and keen eye in completing this project.

chapter one

It was the burst of colors on the poster that first caught my eye. Vibrant reds and greens and yellows jumped off the white background. *Oliver!* the poster shouted, *Open Auditions!* Below were the well-known characters from the Charles Dickens tale: an orphan, bowl in outstretched hands, and the raggedy outline of Fagin rubbing his hands together.

I knew the story well. Mom and I had first read the book when I was about eight.

I'd seen the movie on DVD at least three or four times. It was Mom's favorite. She loved the music. I did too.

"Awwl-liver!" roared a voice behind me in the hallway of Sainsbury High School. "That is soooo gay!"

I didn't need to turn around to know who it was. Ben Stillman's booming voice seemed to fill the entire school. I had heard it plenty of times on the basketball court. Too many times, in fact.

"Guess all the pansies will be lining up for auditions," Ben snorted. He slapped me on the back between my shoulder blades—a little too hard to be considered friendly.

"Whaddya think, Evans? They could likely use a ballerina like you in the Sainsbury fine-arts fling. You up for it?"

I bristled. My ears burned and my jaw clenched as anger surged inside me. Ben Stillman was a teammate, but he was also a jerk. Loud, obnoxious, overconfident and just plain stupid. Just because the kid could rebound and score inside didn't mean I had to like him.

Ben continued his verbal assault on the *Oliver!* poster. "No doubt Pukas will be lined up for that one," he sneered.

He was referring to Lukas Connor, one of his prime bullying targets. Lukas lived a couple of blocks from our house. We had hung out regularly all through elementary school. We'd actually had a lot of fun back then, dressing up in costumes and creating comedy and dance routines that we performed for our parents. Those times with Lukas were some of my best memories.

But Lukas and I didn't spend much time together these days. By middle school, I had become pretty much obsessed with sports. Luke simply wasn't an athletic kid. He was into things I wasn't, like science fiction, chess and theater. Especially theater. Lukas still loved to act and dance and sing. And because of that, he was picked on by a lot of kids at Sainsbury, especially Ben Stillman.

"Yeah, Luke will likely be a star some day," I replied wearily, wishing I hadn't encouraged Stillman to talk about Lukas. Even though we didn't hang out anymore, I still thought Lukas was okay. So what if he liked drama? Who did that hurt?

"A star *queen,* that is," Ben Stillman shot back. "Kind of a *queer* one, that boy."

I cringed. By now I was desperate to change the subject. "You ready for practice?" I asked Stillman. "I hear Coach is super serious this year."

"Coach" was Coach Wayne Williams. During the summer he had been promoted to head coach of the Eagles, our school's senior varsity basketball team. Stillman and I, along with half a dozen other juniors, were moving up to the senior squad with the coach. Our group was good. We had won the city junior varsity championship and finished second at regionals the previous spring. Now Coach Williams wanted the big prize: the regional senior varsity championship. Each one of us had already begun to feel the pressure.

"Whatever," Stillman replied. "I'm more than ready for Sainsbury ball."

I hated the tone of Stillman's voice. Ben was six-foot-five and about two hundred pounds. He was one of the top-rated grade eleven basketball players in the entire region. In fact, he had been selected to play on the regional all-star team over the past summer. Stillman was good, but not nearly as good as he thought he was. Coach Williams and nearly everybody else around the Sainsbury basketball program babied Stillman and even kissed his butt on a fairly regular basis. Some people referred to Ben as the coach's "meal ticket." I suppose, in a way, they were right.

"Did you do all your summer workouts?" I asked Stillman. "Some of that stuff was pretty tough."

"Yeah, right!" Stillman snorted. "Like I had time for that. Summer for me is about *all-star* ball, dude, not running suicide sprints for Coach."

With that, Stillman turned slowly and ambled toward the gym door. I wasn't in any hurry to follow him. I'd get enough of Stillman's act on the court. I didn't need any extra helpings.

Although I couldn't stand the kid, I also couldn't help but be a bit envious. He was three inches taller than me and at least thirty pounds heavier. Whenever we battled under the boards—and that was often during practice—I usually got the worst of it. But Stillman didn't spend enough time in the gym. His shot wasn't as reliable as it could be. He was also prone to foul trouble, because he didn't concentrate on moving his feet on defense. So even though he was a regional all-star, he and I had actually played about the same number of minutes last season. We had each averaged about twelve points a game as tenth-graders. But while college recruiters had already started sending Ben mail, no one seemed to have noticed me. Stillman's name seemed to be in the newspaper on a regular basis. I was still waiting for my first mention.

I focused again on the bright poster on the hallway wall. *Oliver!* was a great choice for a school drama production. I wondered what it would be like to be on stage, performing in front of hundreds of people. Probably a lot like playing in a big basketball game.

I turned away and headed down the hallway toward the gym. Better get focused on practice. Coach Williams would be waiting.

chapter two

I was only vaguely aware of the beeping of my alarm clock. For a few minutes I drifted in and out of dreams of sinking jumpshots from the precise point where the sideline meets the baseline. Fans rose to their feet behind me. Popcorn spilled out of tubs. The ball swished cleanly through the net.

"Kyle!" my mother's voice cut through the morning fog. "You're late, kid. It's already seven o'clock. Better get up."

I scrambled out of bed. Seven o'clock! Practice started in half an hour. Coach would be pissed if I was late. I didn't need Coach being angry with me today or any other day. I frantically slipped on the bright red Nike shorts that lay on the floor beside my bed. Then I grabbed my Sainsbury gym bag. My powder-blue Converse hightops were inside. I tossed the backpack holding my school books over one shoulder. Then I paused briefly in the bathroom to brush my teeth and splash some cold water on my face.

I hurried down the stairs. "No time," I said before Mom could get in a single word about breakfast. "I'll grab something after practice."

"Love you," she yelled as I rushed down the front steps. I waved my right arm behind my head in her general direction. I was being rude, but Mom would understand.

Two blocks down Albion Street, I flipped open my cell phone. I was relieved to see it was still only 7:20 AM. Everything would be fine. It only took five minutes to get to school from here. Less if I picked up the pace.

Looking down at my phone, I nearly stumbled into Lukas Connor, who was also rushing toward the school. Lukas was slight and blond. Today he wore black dress pants and hard shiny shoes. His tight-fitting sweater was decorated with a turquoise-and-black diamond design. Definitely different from the oversize T-shirts and baggy jeans most guys at Sainsbury throw on every morning.

"Hey, Kyle," Luke said quietly. "You're heading in early."

"Yeah," I smiled. "Practice. You know."

Luke nodded. We walked along in silence. It had been awhile since we'd spoken, and I was finding it a little awkward. Which was weird, considering we had spent almost every day together as little kids. But those days seemed like a long time ago.

"What about you?" I finally asked. "You sucking up for straight A's this morning or what?"

Lukas smiled, his pale thin face reddening slightly. "Nah. I'm auditioning for the school show."

My mind flashed back to the poster I had seen the day before in the Sainsbury hallway. Of course. Lukas was headed in to audition for *Oliver!* He'd probably get a big part too. Even though a lot of the jocks thought Lukas was weird, everybody had to admit he was talented. And I knew from our days putting on plays for our parents that the kid was a born ham once he got up on stage.

"Well, um, break a leg, I guess," I said.

Lukas beamed. "You too. But you don't really say that in basketball, do you?"

I laughed. "Later," I said as we approached the Sainsbury High parking lot. "Later," Lukas replied. We took off in separate directions. I headed to the south wing, where the school's gym was located.

Lukas went to the north wing and the community theater.

I pushed through the double doors of the gymnasium. The clock on the wall above Coach Williams's office showed 7:31 AM. I headed directly for the locker room but was halted by the sound of the coach knocking on the window of his office. Coach Williams was beckoning to me. I gulped and headed inside. Whatever this was about, it couldn't be good.

"Evans, what time does that clock out there say?" he asked. His forehead wrinkled below his thick black hair. His voice was sterner than usual.

My shoulders slumped and my ears burned. "Just after seven thirty," I replied.

"What it says is seven thirty-two," the coach barked. "That's two minutes after you're supposed to be out there on the court, dressed and ready for practice like the rest of your teammates."

"I know, Coach, sorry...," I sputtered.

"Save it." Coach Williams cut me off. "Be on time. That's your responsibility as a member of this team. Now go join the guys on the track outside. And for showing up late, you can take an extra lap."

I nodded in guilty agreement and hurried into the locker room. I quickly put on my basketball shoes and my blue-and-white reversible Sainsbury practice jersey; then I headed for the doors that led to the school track. Great, the sun's barely up, and already Coach is pissed at me.

Out on the track, the other members of the Sainsbury senior varsity basketball team were jogging casually around the four-hundred-meter track. It was a crisp late September morning. The dew on the grass was being sucked away as the sun warmed the entire schoolyard, filling the air with a refreshing mist. I jumped onto the track and hurried to join Sammy Curtis, who had already completed a lap.

"Hey, what's up, K-Man?" Sammy grinned, his bright red curls bouncing as he ran. He looked like the high-school jock version of Ronald McDonald.

Sammy was my best friend, both on the basketball court and off. We had pretty much learned the sport together in my driveway, playing nonstop summer games of one-on-one. He was about six feet tall with an angular bony frame. Although I was two inches taller and much more refined as a basketball player, Sammy nearly made up the difference in sheer hustle and heart. I enjoyed playing with Sammy and was really pleased not to have to play against him. He was a tough kid and a great athlete.

"Nice of you to show up, K-Mart." The sarcastic remark came from Ben Stillman, who was lumbering down the track a few feet behind us. I detested that nickname, mostly because Stillman had coined it. I knew Ben meant it in a nasty way, even though it didn't make any sense. Why call a kid the name of a discount department store? Typical Stillman. Stupid.

"Hey, Evans, we're taking this season seriously," Stillman continued. "So next time, set your alarm." He turned on the speed and whizzed past Sammy and me.

"I can't stand that guy," Sammy said, echoing my thoughts. "If he was half as good as he thinks he is, he'd have skipped high school and gone straight to the NBA."

I laughed. It was true. The only thing bigger than Ben Stillman's mouth was his ego. He was a good player. Probably the best player on the Sainsbury team if I had to be honest about it. But he wasn't *that* good.

"I'll get here on time as soon as you start practicing your jump shot," I fired back at Ben as he ran ahead. Everybody on the team knew that if Stillman could become a decent shooter, he'd be a can't-miss college player. But everybody also knew that he was bone lazy.

It was a good line. Sammy laughed hard and flashed me a wide smile. But it was also extremely poor timing. I hadn't realized that Coach Williams was within earshot when I'd said it.

"Evans, get over here!" the coach yelled.

I felt my stomach flip. What an idiot I was today.

"Son, I gave you a warning about showing up late this morning," Coach Williams said sternly. "Apparently it didn't have much effect if you still think it's something to joke about."

"No, Coach," I responded weakly.

"No, what?" the coach said. "No, it didn't have an effect? Or no, being late to practice isn't something to joke about?"

I was confused and flustered. "Being late isn't funny, Coach," I babbled, now completely embarrassed. I could see my teammates straining to hear what we were saying.

"You're right," the coach said. "And just to prove that point, you're going to be suiting up with the second five today. Curtis will take your place. Work your way back to the first string by being on time tomorrow."

I was stunned. I'd been a first-team player for Coach Williams since ninth grade. Now Sammy was going to take my place in the first unit for practice. Great for Sammy. Not so great for me.

There was nothing I could do or say. I pulled my white practice jersey over my head and reversed it. I was now wearing blue, the second-team color. Coach Williams spoke to Sammy, who slowly changed his jersey to the white side. Sammy glanced back at me, shrugged and gave me an awkward smile. There was no way I could be mad at my buddy for this.

The team returned to the gym and began running through some warm-up drills. Coach paired Ben Stillman with me for a defensive shuffle drill. I dribbled the ball first. Stillman shuffled along closely in his defensive crouch. "Nice work today," he smirked. "Maybe by the end of the day, you'll be on the third team."

I didn't respond even though I was furious. I knew that if I threw the ball at Stillman's head, like I really wanted to, Coach would go ballistic. I just had to eat it for now. Tomorrow I would wake up on time.

chapter three

The phone beside my desk rang that night as I finished up some math homework. I got it on the second ring. "Is Kyle there?" said the soft voice on the other end.

"This is him."

"Hey, it's Lukas."

I was surprised. He hadn't phoned me for years.

"Hey," I replied. "How did the auditions go?"

"That's what I wanted to talk to you about," Lukas said. "Do you have a minute?"

Lukas went on to explain that Ms. Lawson, the Sainsbury drama teacher, was looking for actors for *Oliver!* The production featured an orphan and a gang of boy-criminals. But there was a shortage of boys interested in onstage roles. And apparently none of the girls wanted to be cast as boys. Ms. Lawson was desperate. Lukas would no doubt get a big part, but there were still lots of other roles to be filled.

"You could have a part too, Kyle," he suggested.

"Me? Get serious! I can't act." I laughed.

"I think you're forgetting about those plays we used to put on," Lukas said. "You were awesome. You were great at accents, and your singing voice isn't bad—"

"That was years ago," I countered. "I'm not into that kind of stuff anymore."

An awkward silence hung on the phone line.

"Well, if you change your mind...," Lukas said. The disappointment in his voice was unmistakable. "I think you should give it a shot. You'd be great."

"Not going to happen," I said firmly. "I'm just not into it."

"Okay, then. Sorry to bother you, Kyle."

"You're not bothering me, Lukas. It's just...Well, I'm into other stuff now."

"Okay, see you around."

"See you." I hung up the phone, feeling really awful but not quite understanding why. Why should I feel bad? It's not as if Lukas and I hung out anymore.

At supper, Mom asked who had called.

"Just Lukas," I replied.

"Lukas Connor?" she said, surprise in her voice. "That's great, Kyle. You two haven't hung out for a while. He's such a nice boy."

"We're not hanging out now," I said sharply. "He just phoned me, that's all."

Mom didn't bring up the subject again. Dinner was pretty quiet since Dad was working late at the newspaper. It was nearing election time. My father was a reporter for the *Bulletin*. He always had to put in extra hours whenever elections rolled around.

I went to bed that night feeling guilty. Guilty for being late to practice. Guilty for disappointing Lukas. Guilty for getting irritated with Mom.

Now that I had time to think about it, something about Lukas asking me to be in the drama production really bothered me. Why did Lukas want me to be in the show? Why was he trying to be all buddy-buddy now, after years of not hanging around together? Lukas was all right. But he wasn't like the rest of my friends. He was shy. He didn't like sports. He was a little on the feminine side. He didn't really fit into my crowd. I drifted off to sleep, still wondering what it was about the conversation with Lukas that had bothered me so much.

The next morning, I got up as soon as my alarm sounded. I was on my way to school a good fifteen minutes earlier than the previous day. As I hustled up Albion, I noticed Lukas about two blocks ahead. "Hey, Luke," I called. He looked back and waved, but he didn't wait for me.

This time, when I arrived in the locker room only about half the team was there. I dressed quickly, pulling on my basketball shoes and taking the court. It was raining, so we were doing laps in the gym. "Nice to see you ladies all here on time," Coach Williams said sarcastically. He seemed to stare at me for an extra second.

He put us through a tough one-hour practice. Everybody was huffing and bending over when he called us to the center of the court for his final words. "All right, boys," Coach said. "As you know, we only have a few practices before the season begins.

"Before we get into our schedule, I wanted to say a few words about expectations. When I say that, I mean my expectations of you, but more than that. I also mean your expectations of yourselves.

"Boys, we have the potential to be a very good team this year. Maybe even a regional championship team. How far we go depends on how hard you are all willing to work and whether you are willing to make basketball your number one priority outside of school. Is everybody willing to do that?"

Heads nodded all around. I thought about what the coach was saying. Was basketball my number one priority? Well, it was right up there, for sure. But was it higher than my friends and family? Was it higher than Jenna?

Coach was right. Next week was special for all of us. It marked the beginning of our basketball schedule. But it was doubly special for me because it marked the return of Jenna McBride. Jenna and I had seen a lot of each other the previous year, but she and her family had spent the last six months in London. Her father was on an exchange with another college professor from England. The McBrides were coming home this weekend. I couldn't wait to see Jenna. I was hoping she still felt the same way about me after six months apart.

So, yes, basketball was important. But as far as I was concerned it shared top billing with a few other things. I thought it best not to argue with Coach. I had the feeling he wouldn't understand.

chapter four

I waited until Saturday night to call the McBrides' house. I was dying to see Jenna again. We had exchanged e-mails regularly while she was in England. Even so, I was worried that maybe I'd forgotten what she looked like. Or even worse, that she'd forgotten me. Still, I didn't want to seem too desperate.

All I got, though, was the same message that had been on their phone all summer. (I had phoned it a few times just to hear

Jenna's voice.) This time, I left a message for Jenna.

Two hours later, the phone rang. "Kyle? Hi!" The voice on the other end was like an ice-cold drink on a blistering hot day. Jenna didn't sound any different after her six months away. I hoped she didn't feel any different, either.

"Hi!" I replied. "When did you guys get back? I mean, it's good to hear from you."

"We just got in. Can you come over? I can't wait to see you."

It was such a big relief to hear that Jenna felt the same way I did. "I can come right now," I blurted. "I'll be there in five."

My heart pounded as I grabbed my gray hoodie—the one that Jenna always said looked good on me. I stopped in the bathroom to give my hair a brush, even though I knew it would get messed up again when I put on my bike helmet. Why was I so nervous? I had known Jenna for ten years. It wasn't like we hadn't been apart before. But somehow this was different.

I jumped on my mountain bike and pedaled the eight blocks down Albion to Stockport and then up Vera Cruz. I had probably ridden this route a thousand times but never quite this quickly. As I pulled into the McBrides' driveway, Dr. McBride was unloading suitcases from the car. "Hey, Kyle," he said, beaming. "It's good to see you."

"You too," I said. "Did you have a good time in London?"

"It was great—a real life-changing experience. But I think somebody in there missed you quite a bit." He jerked his head toward the house. "Go on in. She's expecting you."

My heart nearly burst through my hoodie as I took the front steps by twos. The door was open, so I just went in. "Jenna?" I called.

"I'm in here!" came a familiar voice from the kitchen. I rounded the corner and took my first look at Jenna in a long time. She jumped out of her chair and rushed around the table, throwing both arms around me in a huge hug. I squeezed back. It was good to feel her so close. It was only then that I realized just how much I had missed her.

Jenna stepped back from me. She hadn't changed much. Her auburn hair had been cut fashionably short. She was a bit taller too. But her face was the same—delicate and heart-shaped. Her broad smile and bright blue eyes illuminated the kitchen.

"It's great to see you," I said, feeling awkward once again.

"You too," she said. I wished I could hold onto this moment—and Jenna—forever.

We quickly started catching up. Jenna had obviously had a fantastic time in London. I felt small pangs of jealousy as she talked about her new English friends and how she'd traveled in Europe with her parents. She'd even seen a few shows in London's theater district. "You wouldn't believe how good the shows are," she said, her eyes opening wide. "I can't wait to tell Lukas. London would be his dream come true."

Jenna, Lukas and I had been best friends throughout elementary school. Even though Lukas and I had drifted apart, he and Jenna had remained close. They shared a love of the theater and had taken some summer acting courses together.

"I talked to Luke this week," I told her. "He's trying out for *Oliver!*"

"I love that show," she said. "Luke should get a part, no problem."

"No doubt," I replied. "They're so desperate for guys, he even asked me to try out."

"And?"

"And what?" I said.

"Are you going to do it?"

"No. I'm pretty busy with basketball. I'm just not into theater the way he is."

"Oh, come on, you'd be great," Jenna insisted. "You should think about it at least."

What seemed like only a couple of minutes later, Dr. McBride tapped on the door of the kitchen and then stepped inside.

"Hey, I know you two haven't seen each other for a while. But it's nearly eleven, and we've all got a bit of jet lag."

I couldn't believe it. Jenna and I had been in the kitchen for nearly two hours, just talking. "I'd better get going," I said, taking the hint. "What are you doing tomorrow?"

"Hanging out with you, I hope," Jenna said, giving me a sweet smile.

We walked to the McBrides' front door and stepped outside. Jenna turned and faced me. We leaned together and shared the first kiss we'd had in half a year. "I missed you so much," she said softly.

"Me too."

I felt like I could have flown home that night. Everything in my world seemed to be better now that Jenna was back.

When I got to the McBrides' house the next morning, her mom answered the door. "Hello, Kyle. It's nice to see you again." She smiled warmly. "Jenna's in the backyard."

I walked around the side of the house and through the white wooden gate. Jenna didn't hear me coming. She was standing near the green picnic table and singing to a completely empty lawn. "'As long as he needs me...,'" she sang. Her voice was terrific.

After listening to her for a few seconds, I cleared my throat. Jenna spun around and grinned. "How long have you been there?" she said. "I've been practicing."

"For *Oliver!*" I replied. "I recognize the tune. The bad guy's girlfriend sings it, right?" Jenna would be perfect for the part of Nancy.

She nodded. "I called Ms. Lawson at home this morning and asked her if I could get a late audition," Jenna explained. "She's going to try me out for Nancy on Monday. So I've got some work to do."

"You'll be great," I said. I meant it.

"I've been thinking about what you told me last night," Jenna said. "You should try out for *Oliver!* too. It would be awesome for you and Luke and me to be in a show."

"Not interested," I said. "I've got basketball. It's pretty hard-core this year."

"But you guys practice mostly in the morning. The rehearsals are all after school. You could do both. And you'd be really good at it."

"I don't know," I said doubtfully.

"Okay, how about this?" Jenna said. "Just audition. See what happens. It doesn't mean you have to take the part if you get one. What could it hurt?"

Somehow, Jenna was much more convincing than Lukas had been. And besides, if I did get into the show, there was now an obvious fringe benefit: Jenna and I could spend a lot of time together.

"All right," I said, throwing up my hands in mock surrender. "I give up. I'll audition."

We spent the rest of the afternoon going over Jenna's lines for the character Nancy. In most of the scenes, I had to play either Fagin or her boyfriend, Bill Sykes.

I was only reading the lines off a script that Jenna had borrowed from Lukas, but it felt good to work at something other than sports or school.

chapter five

"You're what?" Sammy said incredulously. "Dude, tell me you're kidding, right?"

I shook my head. "No, I'm trying out," I said matter-of-factly. "What's the big deal? I probably won't have a sniff at a part."

"So, why even try out then?" Sammy asked. "You're not all of a sudden interested in the fine arts are you?"

As he spoke, Sammy arched his arms above his head and bent his bony knees into a plié.

"Give it a rest," I said. "Look, there's a good reason I'm doing this. Jenna's back and she's probably in the show, and..."

"Ahhhh," Sammy said. "Now I get it. I knew there had to be more to it."

I decided to let the subject drop. I didn't want to tell Sammy that I actually enjoyed the theater. I didn't need any extra grief. Coach Williams had been on my butt last week about being late. I was nervous about practice this week. The season was tipping off Friday with a home game against Davidson, our arch rivals.

Coach had only kept me on the second string for one practice, during which Sammy had pretty much played me back onto the starting five by screwing up nearly every play in our offense. If I didn't know better, I'd suspect he'd been tanking on purpose in order to get me back on the first unit. But Sammy would never do that.

He wanted badly to be first string, maybe too badly. That desire had made him nervous around Coach. There had been several instances when Sammy ran one play while the rest of the team ran another.

Still, I was relieved when coach put our first-team offense on the floor against the second-team defense. I was back in my usual small-forward slot. I was proud of being a starter in my eleventh-grade year. I was determined to keep that spot even if it meant setting my alarm an hour earlier every day.

"We're going to focus on our four-set today," Coach barked as we prepared to go through our halfcourt offense. "Unless we get a big surprise from Davidson, I expect to run this set all game on Friday. So let's make sure we know it cold."

Everybody nodded in agreement, including me, but inside I was disappointed. The four-set was the name for a series of plays which featured Ben Stillman, our power forward or "four" player. That meant Coach was planning to go heavily with Stillman against Davidson—again. No wonder people referred to Stillman as our meal ticket.

For the next half hour, we ran plays through Stillman. Stillman posting up. Stillman going backdoor for a lob. Stillman coming off a screen for a jumpshot. That last one was difficult for me to swallow. Stillman's jumper was likely the worst on the team, but the coach always called his number far more often than mine.

"Okay, let's work on the three-set," Coach declared. Finally, I thought. I'm going to get a few more touches here.

We ran the three-set with me shooting the ball for all of five minutes. I hit every shot I took. I wondered if Coach even noticed. He seemed far more preoccupied with Sammy's defense than with anything I was doing.

That was pretty much it for practice. We had only an hour and it usually went by quickly. On our way into the locker room,

Ben Stillman was right behind me. "Get set to watch me shoot a whole lot this week," he said quietly in my ear. "Coach likes to call my number. It's going to be that way all year."

I couldn't believe what I was hearing, even from Stillman. Maybe he was right. Maybe Coach would be calling his number a lot this year. But why tell me about it? If you looked up the definition of *jerk* in the dictionary, Stillman's picture would be there.

"We'll see, Stillman," I replied. "He won't keep calling it you keep missing."

Anger flashed across Stillman's broad face. His dark eyes were fiery. "I'll get more shots in every game than you get in any practice, Evans," he said. "Coach knows who the stud on this team is."

I shook my head and looked at Ben. Did this guy actually believe the things he said? "Whatever, man," I replied tersely. "What's it like being the president of your own fan club, anyway?"

Stillman swore at me under his breath. I headed for my locker, half expecting him to come after me. For some reason he didn't. Instead he turned and headed to his locker stall in between Kurt Flatley's and Joey Armstrong's. Kurt and Joey were a pair of second-stringers who always had his back.

I saw Jenna in the cafeteria at lunch. Between spoonfuls of vegetable beef soup, she reminded me that the final tryout session for *Oliver!* was this afternoon. Ms. Lawson had agreed to hold an extra session for Jenna and anybody else who wanted to audition.

"Nervous?" Jenna asked playfully.

"Nah, it's no big deal," I lied. Inside, I was already feeling butterflies. I hadn't performed in front of anybody since fifth grade. Even then it was only Jenna and Luke and our parents. This afternoon, I would have to read lines for Ms. Lawson, the parents who were on the selection jury and the other cast members. Sure I was nervous.

"I've got to go see Mr. Riley before lunch is over," Jenna said. "He's got a ton of math for me to catch up on. He's making me do all the work I missed when I was away."

"Are you serious?" I said. I hated math. Not only was it dull, it was also difficult. I couldn't imagine doing more than I already did.

"See you at four in the theater." Jenna smiled.

I waved as she got up and headed for the cafeteria door. What had I got myself into? I didn't even know what part I was trying out for.

Then again, who was I kidding? What did it matter? I wasn't going to get a part, anyway. I would go, deliver a few lines, and they'd hook me off the stage. Case closed.

Even so, I spent a good portion of my geography and Spanish classes that after-noon stewing about the auditions. My legs felt weak and my throat was dry as I walked down the hallway toward the theater after my final class of the day.

There were only half a dozen kids in the mostly empty theater. Ms. Lawson and two parent-jurors, neither of whom I recognized, sat in the front row. I could hit free throws in front of hundreds of people on the basketball court, but I felt myself growing nervous in front of just a handful of people in the little theater. Was it too late to run?

"Kyle, this is a surprise," Ms. Lawson exclaimed. "Lukas told me he asked you to try out, but I thought you didn't want to."

"It's kind of a surprise to me too," I said, eyeing Jenna. She smiled at me from behind Ms. Lawson and mouthed the words *You'll be fine*.

Jenna was first up, and she was awesome. She ran through her lines in a scene with Luke, who was playing Fagin. Her English accent was perfect, something she had obviously learned during her time in London.

And her acting, as she pleaded with Fagin to spare Oliver from a life of crime, was extremely realistic. I was impressed.

"Okay, Jenna, that was very nice," said Ms. Lawson. "Now, I'd like to hear you sing."

Sing? What did Ms. Lawson mean? Surely you didn't have to sing as part of the audition. I hadn't bargained on this.

To make matters worse, Jenna was near perfect as she sang "As Long as He Needs Me." She absolutely nailed it. And even though she was supposed to be impartial, Ms. Lawson stood up and clapped when Jenna was done. "That was wonderful," she cried. "Great to have you back, Jen!"

I smiled at Jenna. I was feeling so good for her that I almost forgot about my own nerves. Almost. Two kids later, it was my turn.

Ms. Lawson handed me a script. "I'd like you to read for the part of the Artful Dodger," she smiled. "Are you familiar with the story?"

"Yes," I said. "But I haven't practiced the—"

"No worries, Kyle," Ms. Lawson said soothingly. "I assume you can read, right?"

I laughed. The drama teacher's gentle manner and sense of humor had managed to relax me. Now I was just in a mild panic instead of a full-blown one.

I read with Jake Barnett, a small blond boy who had obviously landed the part of Oliver. It was good casting. The kid was so scrawny and pitiful-looking that even I believed he could have been a ragged orphan.

The reading actually went pretty well. "Fine job, Kyle," Ms. Lawson said.

"Thanks," I replied, starting down the steps at the side of the stage.

"Wait, Kyle," she said. "We still need to hear you sing."

Sing? Now? In front of all these people? Not a great idea.

"I don't think so," I mumbled, looking down at the floor. "I mean, I haven't prepared anything."

"Never mind that," Ms. Lawson said. "We just need to get an idea about any hidden talents you might have. This is mostly a dramatic production, but there will be four or five songs. Which ones we choose will depend on which of our actors can sing. I'd like you to try singing with the piano player. Does this key work for you?"

Mrs. Davis, the Sainsbury music teacher, played a few bars of "Consider Yourself." I knew the song from the movie production of *Oliver!* It was a lively tune in which the Artful Dodger welcomes Oliver to the pickpocketing gang.

"Sure," I said, not feeling the least bit sure about either the key or my performance.

Mrs. Davis started again, playing the brief introduction to the piece. Before I had much time to think, I had to begin. "'Consider yourself, at home...,'" I started.

"Okay, hang on, Kyle," Ms. Lawson yelled from her seat. I couldn't believe she was stopping me already. Was I that bad?

"That sounded fine," she said. "But this is the theater. You need to project. I need to hear you sing full-out."

I nodded. I thought I had been singing loudly, but the piano had drowned me out. Mrs. Davis began again. What the heck. I'm just going to belt it.

"'Consider yourself, at home,'" I sang. "'Consider yourself, one of the family...'"

I don't know quite how it happened, but within seconds I was really getting into it. I was singing full voice. I even began mimicking some of the dance moves the actor playing Dodger had performed in the movie.

After I had finished, Ms. Lawson and Mrs. Davis spoke briefly to each other and then to the jurors. "That was good, Kyle," Ms. Lawson said. "We'll be in touch."

After the elation of the performance, her reaction was kind of a letdown. What did "good" mean? Did it mean I would get a part in the production? Or did it mean "pretty good for a dumb jock basketball player"?

"Well?" I asked Jenna and Lukas as we walked out of the theater. "How do you think it went?"

"Are you kidding?" Lukas said, his blue eyes opening wide. "You were awesome. I knew you'd be great."

"You amaze me," Jenna smiled. "I think Ms. Lawson was blown away."

Inside, I wasn't so sure. Jenna and Lukas were probably just being kind. They could tell I had been nervous. After walking partway home with them, I continued by myself up Albion. I was confident that at least I hadn't embarrassed myself on stage. But I was also feeling confused. What had started out as a bit of a goof had suddenly become important to me. I had missed performing in the years since Lukas and I had been elementary school hambones. And for the first time I admitted it to myself: I really wanted a part in this show.

chapter six

The telephone rang just as we were finishing supper.

"Leave it," Mom said. She hated it when our rare family dinners were interrupted. But my father couldn't bear to let it ring. Who knew when it might be one of his editors calling about a breaking news story? Although he wasn't quite finished eating, he got up, walked quickly into the kitchen and picked up the receiver.

"Just a minute, please," he said. "Kyle, it's for you."

I jumped up and grabbed the phone.

"Hello."

"Kyle?"

"Yes."

"This is Ms. Lawson. I just wanted to call and tell you how much we enjoyed your audition today. You did great. I had no idea you were hiding such talents under that basketball uniform."

I blushed. "Thanks," I said.

"The reason I'm calling is because we think you'd make a great Artful Dodger," she continued. "But I needed to speak with you first and make sure you're up for the challenge. It's going to require a major time commitment. If you want it, that is."

I felt stunned. The Artful Dodger? I hadn't expected to get even a bit part in *Oliver!* let alone one of the main roles. This was really exciting.

"Sure," I said. "I mean, yeah. I can put the time in."

"I'm worried about your involvement in basketball," Ms. Lawson said. "Is that going to get in the way of the show? You know, you absolutely have to be at rehearsals, Kyle. We can't make exceptions for anybody or anything. This show is a big deal. We have rehearsals after school from Monday through Thursday for the next six weeks. We sometimes rehearse on weekends too. The production runs in mid-November. There will be several shows for the community as well as for other schools. And of course we perform for the Sainsbury student body and their families.

"And Kyle, judging from your singing today, we're thinking of having you sing a number," Ms. Lawson said. "Are you up for that?"

Sing a number? By myself? On stage?

I heard my voice answering, even before I had time to weigh the consequences, "Yeah, sure."

Although it was a major time commitment, the show's practice times worked out almost perfectly with basketball. The team practiced every morning from Monday through Thursday. Most of our games were on Friday nights. There shouldn't be much of a conflict at all.

"So, Kyle, can we count on you?" Ms. Lawson asked.

"Yes," I replied quickly. "That's awesome. See you tomorrow afternoon."

Mom and Dad were both looking at me with puzzled expressions. I hadn't told them anything about the *Oliver!* tryouts. I had planned to, eventually. I had been waiting until I heard whether I got a part. I certainly hadn't expected to find out this soon.

After I explained the phone call to them, a big grin broke across Mom's face. "Wow," she said, grabbing my hand and squeezing it. "I had no idea you were even trying out. I'm so proud of you!"

"Me too," Dad chimed in. "How's this going to work with basketball, though? You know Coach Williams is pretty serious."

"I think it'll be okay," I said. "I mean, our practices don't conflict and neither do our games. I'll talk to Coach about it tomorrow morning."

I had trouble getting to sleep that night because I was so excited. First of all, we were playing Davidson on Friday in our opening game of the season. And second, I had just landed a part in the school play. My grade eleven year was shaping up pretty nicely so far.

I was up like a shot the next morning when the alarm rang at 6:30 AM. As a result, I had enough time to down a couple of pieces of toast, a banana and a glass of orange juice. I even had time to scan the Sports section of the *Bulletin*. I never read the news pages, even though my dad writes for them.

It was only 7:15 AM when I entered the Sainsbury gym. I had planned to arrive early so that I could talk to Coach Williams about my part in *Oliver!* I didn't want him to find out from Ms. Lawson in the staff room or from another student in PE class. Coach was a funny guy. He liked to have control over his players. I was pretty sure he'd want to hear this news from me.

Coach Williams's door was open, but I knocked anyway. He looked up from his desk. He was sipping coffee from a large red mug and poring over some statistics. "What's up, Kyle?" he asked.

"I just wanted to talk to you, Coach," I said, hating the nervous croak in my voice.

"Shoot," Coach Williams replied, leaning back in his chair and locking his hands behind his head.

"I've got a part in the school play," I said. "I just wanted you to know that. It won't interfere with practices and—"

Coach cut me off in mid-sentence. His brow was furrowed. He looked much more annoyed than impressed. "Kyle, you should have checked this out with me first," he said.

I was taken aback by his reaction. What harm did it do to him if I was in the school play? And what did he mean "check it out with him"? What was I, his slave?

"The school play is a huge commitment," Coach said. "But basketball is an even bigger one. Just remember what your top priority is, okay? This year is a real opportunity for us. We've got a chance to do something special on the basketball court. And you're a big part of that, Evans."

I couldn't help but notice that Coach had slipped into using my last name instead of calling me Kyle. Typically, whenever he was mad at a player, he used the kid's last name.

"I'm s-sorry, Coach," I heard myself stuttering. "I should have checked with you first."

Again, he interrupted me. "It's not a problem now, Evans," he said. "Just don't make it a problem, okay?"

I nodded and got up to leave. Coach had already returned to his statistics. He didn't even say good-bye.

I walked out of his office and toward the locker room, feeling dejected. Couldn't Coach just be happy for me? I wasn't planning on ditching the basketball team.

I loved basketball. But there was room in my life for something else too, wasn't there?

At least this morning I was early for practice. I was already in my gear and shooting free throws when the rest of the team rolled in. "You're going to have to get up earlier than that to take my spot." Ben Stillman snickered as he headed past me to the locker room. My only response was a clean swish of the ball from the foul line.

The team ran crisply through the first half of practice, with Coach once again running the four-set and giving Stillman the majority of the shots. Next, he put the starting five in a 2–1–2 zone defense, with me in the middle. Coach told the second-stringers to run Davidson's zone offense against us. As they did that, Coach yelled at the five of us on the first team. "Move your feet, Evans!" he shouted. "C'mon, Stillman, you've got to be there!" he implored as Stillman blew his coverage at the back of the zone, allowing the second-stringers an easy layup. Once again, Stillman seemed to be coasting through defensive practice. It seemed to me that he played hard only when he had the ball in his hands and a chance to score.

"Okay, last time," Coach ordered. "Let's do this right, for once."

We lined up in our 2–1–2 zone, again with me in the middle. The second team moved the ball crisply around the outside, getting it low on the baseline to Pete Freeman. Pete was a six-foot swingman who couldn't shoot well from outside but had some strong moves to the bucket. Stillman jumped out far too hard on Freeman, who used a slick crossover dribble to easily beat Stillman inside. Since we were in a zone, I had to shift from the middle to pick up Freeman going toward the hoop. But as I did that, Pete deftly flipped the ball inside to Sammy Curtis who had cut through the open middle. It was an easy layup for a basket by the second string. Coach Williams didn't like it one bit.

The sound of his clipboard hitting the polished wooden floor echoed across the gym. "Evans!" he screamed, pointing straight at me. "What are you thinking?"

"But Coach...," I began, trying to tell him that I felt I had to cover Freeman since he had beaten Stillman.

"That's enough," Coach yelled. "I don't want to hear any more excuses this morning. We've only got two days until Davidson. That's the team you'll have to defend, not a second string."

By now, everyone could tell that Coach was completely pissed. It hadn't happened all that often, but we had all seen him go off like this before. And none of us wanted to bear the brunt of his anger.

"Evans!" he yelled again at me. "Since you can't play defense properly, take a couple of laps around the track. The rest of you guys, hit the showers."

I headed for the gym door in a state of shock. That play hadn't been my fault, but Coach was taking it out on me. What about Stillman? He was the one who had made the mistake.

As I jogged around the track, a steady rain was falling. But I wasn't thinking about getting wet. I was wondering why Coach had it in for me today. Could it have something to do with my role in *Oliver!*

"So, this is it, everybody." Ms. Lawson beamed from her spot at the front of the theater, as we sat in the first two rows of seats. "This is our cast."

We glanced around at each other with nervous tentative smiles on our faces. I was sitting beside Jenna, who was flanked by Lukas. The rest of the seats were occupied by students whom I knew either vaguely or not at all. There was a charge in the air, a very similar feeling to the first day of basketball practice, right after the final cuts have been made.

"Now, before we get started, I have some business to clear up," Ms. Lawson continued. "Most of it is about commitment. It's very important to the success of our show. I have already spoken with each of you individually about this.

"A big show like this—and believe me, this is a big show—doesn't just happen by you showing up for a few rehearsals. Each of you needs to show up for every rehearsal, unless you're on your deathbed. And that doesn't go just for the cast but also for the technical crew. The sound and lighting and props people will be joining us in the coming weeks.

"My point is, it's a huge team effort. And not one of you here—including the leads—is more important than the team. Is everybody clear on that?"

Everybody nodded in unison.

The first rehearsal was pretty routine, even for a theater rookie like me. We each got a copy of the script and were told to review it silently and highlight our lines and stage cues. Although I had never been part of a show like this before, it all made sense.

We broke into working groups. Since I was Dodger, I was placed in a group with

Lukas. He had landed the part of Fagin, the lovable old criminal who shepherds a band of orphan pickpockets in London. If there was another role that really appealed to me in *Oliver!* it was Fagin. But I was happy for Lukas. I knew he'd be terrific.

Ms. Lawson had us run through our dialogue in certain scenes. From the moment he first read, it was obvious that Lukas had already done plenty of work on his character. Gone was soft-spoken quiet Luke. In his place was jovial, conniving, funny Fagin. I had to marvel at Luke. The kid could really act.

"Good," Ms. Lawson said. "For the next two months, you all must make sure that *Oliver!* is your number one commitment outside schoolwork. Is everybody ready to do that?"

Again, most heads nodded. Except for mine. Was the musical bigger than basketball for me? Bigger than Jenna? I was excited about being part of it, but I couldn't quite go that far.

chapter seven

Friday afternoon couldn't come soon enough for me. But it had absolutely nothing to do with wanting the school week to end. Despite the problems with Coach Williams and Ben Stillman, I was excited about my first season of senior high basketball.

The game against Davidson didn't tip off until seven PM. We didn't have to be in the locker room until six, so most of the guys headed home for a few hours. Not me. I had to report to the theater to help the students who were beginning to prepare the sets.

As I approached the theater, I saw Lukas hanging out with some of the other kids in the cast. I waved at him. "What's up, Kyle?" Luke smiled as he spoke.

"I'm pumped," I replied, glancing at Lukas, who was sitting with Brad Schmidt and Ollie Jacobs. They had landed roles as members of Fagin's gang. Brad and Ollie were skateboarders, with lip-piercings that looked painful. Brad wore his hair in a Mohawk, dyed red on one side and green on the other.

"Pumped for what?" Ollie said with a dry grin. "It's just set design, man. No biggie."

"For the game," I replied. "We got Davidson tonight. It's the start of the season."

Brad and Ollie responded with blank expressions. It was pretty easy to tell that neither was a basketball fan. "You must be excited," Luke said, turning to the others. "Kyle is an awesome basketball player."

"Uhh, cool," Brad said. "Good luck with that."

Their reaction was different from most of the kids I hung out with. My friends knew all about the basketball team.

"So what do we do here?" I asked, looking around the theater.

"Ms. Lawson wants us to go into the art room and pull out those big lengths of backdrop board," Luke said. "We're just hired muscle for today."

I laughed. That was funny, coming from Luke, who was five-foot-nothing and about 120 pounds. I grinned. "Let's do it, then."

It took us about half an hour to lug all the supplies out of the art room and onto the stage. I was surprised by how strong Luke was. By the time we were finished, there were about twenty kids milling about, preparing paints, brushes and other supplies. Ms. Lawson had arrived as well and was dividing the set-makers into working groups.

"By the time you guys see these again, you'll swear you're in the heart of London," she said.

I sat a few rows back in the theater, eating an apple and a granola bar while I watched the set crew go to work. They started by drawing the outlines of buildings on the blank backdrops. Then they penciled in features such as bricks, sloped rooftops and cobblestones. Then, section by section, they began painting the backdrops. I had never realized how much work went into a theater production before it finally hit the stage. I just took it for granted there would be sets and costumes. I never thought about where they came from. It must be the same for somebody who just showed up to watch a basketball game too. They probably had no idea about the hours of practice that went into it before you ever even tried on a uniform.

There was no point heading home and then turning right around and coming back for the game against Davidson. At quarter past five, I got up, said goodbye to Lukas and headed out the theater door. "Good luck," Luke said.

"Thanks, man. I'll probably need it."

In truth, I was a little nervous about the game. Coach Williams had been riding me pretty hard all week. It wouldn't hurt to arrive at the gym early, loosen up and spend some extra time working on my shot.

When I got to the gym, I threw on my practice shorts and a sweatshirt. Then I grabbed a basketball out of the rack in the equipment room and stood directly under one backboard, about a foot away from the rim. It was how I began every solo shooting session: taking several shots, with both my right and left hands, from each side of the floor. My rule was I had to swish one, bank one in, roll one in off the front rim and bounce one in off the back rim. Only then could I slide one step farther out and repeat the entire process.

I didn't even hear Coach Williams come through the gym doors behind me. "Evans, great to see you here early," he said before heading into his office.

It was nice for me to hear something positive from the coach for a change. It had been a rough week bouncing between basketball practice and the musical with homework in between. And Coach had been really uptight all week about tonight's season-opener. You could tell he was already feeling more pressure this season than in any other year I had played for him.

At 6:15 PM the Davidson players began coming through the double doors of the gym. They were wearing the familiar red, white and blue Davidson Dukes varsity jackets, and oozing confidence. Davidson was the other powerhouse team in our district, and their players obviously felt pretty good about themselves. They strode toward the visitors' locker room, laughing and talking loudly.

By then, the rest of my teammates had shown up and joined me in an informal shootaround. "I can't stand those guys," Sammy said after the last Davidson player had entered the locker room. "They think they're an NBA team or something."

The rest of us, even Ben Stillman, nodded as we continued our shooting.

"Okay, guys, let's bring it in!" The harsh blast of Coach Williams's whistle and his stern voice served as a pre-game wake-up call. We took his signal and headed for the locker room. It was almost time for the most important season of my basketball career to begin.

Unlike junior ball, where we all showed up pretty much ready to play, the locker room was a big deal at the senior varsity level. We now got to keep our locker stalls for the entire season. Our names were taped above the spots where we dressed. We were also allowed music. Pete Freeman, the senior who was our sixth man, the first player in off the bench, was in charge of the tunes. As we pulled on our blue-andgold Sainsbury Eagles jerseys and shorts, the locker room filled with the pulsating beats of 50 Cent.

"All right, turn it off!" Only Coach Williams's voice could cut through the bass beat and all the pre-game conversation. "Let's get down to business."

Everybody was silent as Coach strode to the center of the locker room. All eyes were on him. He was dressed in a sharp black suit, blue shirt and gold tie. I hadn't seen the coach in a suit before. It was obvious to all of us how seriously he was taking this season.

"I don't have to tell you guys how big this year is for us," Coach began, his eyes surveying the room. "And of all our games this year, none—not one—is any bigger than this one."

Coach was right on that account. The Davidson Dukes were our arch rivals. The Dukes were defending district champions and had been runners-up at regionals the previous year.

"But this season is different," Coach continued. "It's different because of you guys. You have talent. And tonight we're going to find out whether you have the heart to go along with it."

I looked around the room. Coach had everybody's attention. Ben Stillman looked serious for the first time since practice had begun this fall. Pete Freeman, maybe the most happy-go-lucky kid on our team, had fixed a solemn gaze on the tips of his Nike hightops. Sammy Curtis drew a deep breath and clenched his square jaw. We were all serious and ready to go.

"I know what you are capable of," Coach Williams said. "Now let's go out there and show everybody else."

We all began to chant, first softly and then louder. It was a tradition we had begun as a junior varsity team, and it had simply carried over to the senior team. "Eagles! Eagles! Eagles!" The volume grew, as did the intensity. One by one, we filed out the locker room door and into the gym.

What a difference thirty minutes had made. When we had entered the locker room, the gym had been practically empty. Now there were at least four hundred people in the stands and a cheerleading team on either side of the court. The Sainsbury High School band was set up in one corner of the gym. They were blasting out our school song—"Soar, Eagles, Soar." I could even smell the butter on the popcorn. This was high school basketball— the big time.

We headed out for the pre-game in our new blue-and-gold warm-ups. They had a spread-winged Eagle on the back of the jackets and our numbers on the pants, directly over the right thigh. Big Ben Stillman fired down the lane and jammed the basketball through the hoop to begin our layup drill. The crowd went crazy. I followed up with a two-handed dunk that drew "Oohs" from the little kids in the front row. I remembered being one of those kids not so long ago, watching games at Sainsbury, hoping to catch the eye of one of the players on the court. Finally I was out there on the floor, one of their high-school heroes.

chapter eight

It seemed like only seconds before the referee blew his whistle three times, signaling that it was three minutes to tip-off. Coach called us into the huddle and we stripped off our warm-ups.

"Okay, guys, this is it," Coach Williams said, his voice rising to be heard above the crowd noise. "You're varsity players now. Let's make some noise."

Even though I'd had my share of disagreements with the coach, his words left me pumped up. This was the most excited I had ever felt as an athlete. I put my right hand into the middle of the pack with my teammates. "One, two, three—Eagles!" we screamed.

It felt great to walk onto the court as a starter on the Sainsbury varsity team. I shook hands with Eric Larsen, the senior Davidson forward. I would be matched up against him. I knew Eric pretty well. We had played plenty of summer ball against each other. He nodded at me, and I nodded back. "Good game," I said.

From the opening tip, though, things just didn't go our way. Instead of winning the jump against Davidson center Dave Ansen, Ben Stillman mistimed his leap and the ball went directly to Eric Larsen. He fired it upcourt to Randy Hinks. The Dukes had an uncontested layup just three seconds in.

Instead of getting out to a confident start, that basket seemed to throw the jitters into the entire Sainsbury team. And even though we tried, we couldn't recover. By halftime, Davidson led 30–22. Ben Stillman had missed all five shot attempts he had taken, three of them air balls. I had gone zero-for-two. This certainly wasn't the dream start that Coach Williams or any of us had imagined.

"That was awful," Coach bellowed as soon as our last player had made it into the locker room at halftime. "If I could get them together and dressed in time, I'd put the junior varsity out there for the second half. At least they'd give me some honest effort. You guys look as if you've never played a game before. You look scared. Are you scared?"

Each of us shook his head. I knew we'd had a poor half. I could see that Coach was upset. But I was pretty sure that everybody—even Stillman—was trying as hard as he could.

After going over the mistakes we'd made in the first half—and it took a while—Coach had some final words for us. I wouldn't describe it as a pep talk. Not really. "Now, unless you all are ready to go out and give me a complete effort," he yelled, "then there are going to be major changes come Monday. Do we understand each other?"

I gulped. I wondered what he meant, exactly, by "changes."

The second half was much better for us. Our nerves had settled somewhat. We began to work the ball around the perimeter, into the post and then back out, just the way Coach had shown us in practice.

With one minute left, we had erased Davidson's lead, and the score was tied 40-40. We had possession of the ball. Coach Williams signaled for a time-out.

"Okay, guys. That's more like it," Coach said. "You had me worried for a while."

The coach pulled out his whiteboard with the basketball key on it. With a blue marker, he drew the play he wanted us to run for the rest of the game. "Let's work our four-up and get Stillman the ball," he said. "Ben, you drive and look to dish if you get tied up. Okay?"

We all nodded. Hands went into another huddle. "Eagles!" We exploded onto the court.

Layne Dennis, our senior point guard, brought the ball down the floor. He reversed it to Pete Freeman on the weakside wing. Freeman waited for Stillman to cross to the high post; then he delivered the pass perfectly to the hand that was farthest from the defender.

Ben gathered the ball, faked left and then spun right, driving the lane. He elevated into the key and soared toward the rim. Meanwhile, Eric Larsen slid over to pick up Stillman, leaving me wide open under the basket. But the pass never came. Stillman crashed into Larsen, and the whistle blew. "Shooting two!" the referee shouted.

The Sainsbury crowd roared. Ben Stillman was going to the free-throw line with thirty-one seconds left and a chance to put us ahead.

Ben strode to the line. The rest of us found a place in the lane, playing for the rebound. "First one's dead," the ref said, reminding everyone that there was no rebound on the initial free throw. Ben released the ball awkwardly, and it bounced off the rim. No good.

I gazed over at Stillman. The guy was a goof, and he had a huge opinion of himself, but after four years of playing together I could tell when he was nervous. And he was definitely nervous now. "One shot!" the referee yelled. Ben cradled the basketball, bent his legs and released it. The orange sphere bounced softly around the rim, and this time it fell in. Stillman had made one of two and we were up 41–40.

Davidson called a quick time-out. In the huddle, our coach gave Stillman a pat on the back. "Way to put us ahead." He grinned. "Now listen up, everybody. The ball is likely going to Larsen. Kyle, make sure you don't let him get by you. Okay?"

I nodded. I knew that Davidson would try to find Eric Larsen on this play. Larsen was one of their best shooters and definitely the Dukes' top performer in the clutch.

I left the huddle determined not to let Larsen get away from me. I knew the Dukes would be setting screens for him. "Tell me what's happening, okay?" I said to my teammates loudly as we took the floor. "Let me know about the screens."

Sure enough, the Dukes were intent on running Larsen through a maze before he got the ball. I managed to slip under the first pick set for him, but the second screen proved more difficult. It was Dave Ansen, the plodding Davidson center. Ansen wasn't particularly skilled at anything, except for setting bone-jarring screens.

It might have been okay had Ben been talking to me on defense. But as Ansen set a blind off-ball screen for Eric Larsen, I had no idea what was coming. Whether he saw it developing or not, Ben Stillman never said a word. As Larsen cut hard around

Ansen, I followed. My shoulder crashed dead-on into the larger Davidson player. I was rocked backward at least three feet. I felt the taste of blood in my mouth from a collision with Ansen's elbow.

But what happened next really hurt. Eric Larsen had sprung open off that screen. Ben Stillman was at least a foot behind him trying desperately to catch up. Larsen took a perfect pass from his point guard and laid the ball cleanly into the basket. It was 42–41 for Davidson with just ten seconds remaining.

We had one time-out left, which Layne Dennis wisely called. In the huddle, Coach Williams was livid. "Don't you guys ever talk out there?" he screamed, eyeing both me and Stillman. "That hoop was way too easy."

I felt about two inches tall rather than the six-foot-two listed in the game program. Stillman, meanwhile, was simply sneering at me. Like it was somehow all my fault.

"Okay, boys, let's concentrate," Coach said. "Let's run the same thing as last time. Let's run our four-set, high post from the weak side. Pete, you get the ball to Ben and let him create, okay?"

Freeman inbounded the basketball into Dennis and then headed quickly down-court. Once he reached the baseline, he sprinted back to the offside wing, where he caught a crisp pass from Dennis. Freeman waited for Stillman to cut and then delivered the ball on target.

There were six seconds left when Ben cut toward the hoop, again beating Dave Ansen. But once again, Eric Larsen slid over to pick up Stillman on the drive. I was wide open under the hoop with my hands extended. All Stillman had to do was dump it down to me for the winning basket. But instead he held on to it, thudding directly into Larsen. The two players collided and hit the floor. Ben bounced up and headed toward the free-throw line. But the referee stretched out his left hand, fist clenched, signaling an offensive foul. That was it. The game was over. Davidson had won 42-41.

The rest of the Dukes mobbed Larsen, who had drawn the charge from Stillman to win the game. Meanwhile, everybody in an Eagles uniform looked dejected. Nobody more so than Coach Williams, who was the first to shake hands with the Dukes and head into the locker room.

"Okay, guys, listen up," the coach said after we had all taken a seat. The body language in the locker room told a sad story. Players slumped in their stalls and stared down at the cold tile floor. "That was a tough loss. And worse yet, it was a game we should have won. If you guys had played anywhere close to your potential in the first half, we would have breezed past these guys.

"Let's put this one behind us," he continued. "But let's learn from it. This is senior varsity ball now. You can't afford to be unprepared mentally or physically.

Today, you guys weren't ready mentally when the opening whistle blew."

I didn't disagree with what Coach was saying. None of us, myself included, had been very sharp at the start of the game.

Glancing down at the score sheet, which had just been handed to him by our manager, Coach cleared his throat. "Stillman, twenty-one points. Fifteen after the break. Nice game."

Ben Stillman's face brightened considerably. He smiled at Coach. "Thanks," he said.

Listening to them was a little hard to take. Yes, Stillman had scored twenty-one, but I thought he should have had forty given all the chances he'd had. Plus, he was playing against the much slower Ansen. And besides, he had blown the last two plays of the game. He had missed a free throw and then committed the charge that cost us the win.

I hurried to pull on my sweatpants and varsity jacket. It was nearly nine o'clock, and some of the guys were going out for a pizza. I just wanted to get home. This game had left a bad taste in my mouth.

"Evans," the coach called as I headed toward the gym door. "I need to talk to you a minute."

Startled, I followed him into his office. "Close the door," he said.

"What's up?" I asked, by now feeling anxious. All the guys would be wondering what was going on.

"Five-for-thirteen," he said, reciting my shooting stats for the night. "You can do better than that, kid."

I gulped. "Yeah, Coach," I acknowledged. "I think I was a little nervous out there. First game and all."

The coach fixed his gray eyes directly on mine. "Just as long as nerves is all it is," he said.

I had no idea what he was talking about. "I don't understand," I said.

"Evans, do you know what burning the candle at both ends means?" Coach said.

I nodded. "It means you're spreading yourself too thin."

"Correct," Coach said. "And I'm concerned you're doing that by being involved in this theater thing."

Now I understood what the coach was getting at, but I was also getting angry. My acting had nothing to do with how I had shot the ball tonight. And besides, I had gone five-for-eleven in the second half, nearly fifty percent. I knew Ben Stillman had taken more than twice as many shots as me and scored just twenty-one points to my ten. All he'd managed in the first half were six free throws. But Coach had said "good game" to him.

"I don't think so, Coach," I said.

"Well, let's make sure, Evans," he shot back. "If you're going to remain a starter for me, I need a one hundred percent commitment. Do you understand?"

"Yes, Coach" I said firmly.

As I left the coach's office, I was pissed. Remain a starter? What did that mean?

And why was I the one being delivered the ultimatum when it was the whole team that had lost? Why did Ben Stillman, who blew the game, get an "atta-boy" while I got dumped on?

Sammy Curtis was waiting for me outside the coach's office. "What was that all about?" he asked as we made our way through the gym parking lot.

"Coach doesn't think I'm giving one hundred percent," I said. "He thinks I'm too busy with *Oliver!* It's complete crap."

Sammy didn't say anything for a few seconds. "Why don't you just quit?" he finally said.

"Quit basketball?" I asked. "Are you serious?"

"I meant the show," Sammy said. "Obviously, you're not quitting hoops. But I don't get why you want to hang around with all those theater geeks anyway."

Now I was really pissed. Sammy was my friend and a good guy, but he was just as bad as Coach. I wanted to tell Sammy that

I liked theater almost as much as basketball, and that the guys in the show were actually pretty cool. But something stopped me from speaking.

We had reached the corner of Albion and Smith, where we had to go our separate ways. "See you at shootaround." He smiled.

"Yeah, okay," I mumbled.

I had completely forgotten about shootaround, the informal session Coach held every Saturday during the season. It was a day when players showed up, shot a couple of hundred shots and then scrimmaged for two hours. It wasn't mandatory, but Coach was always there. You just knew that if you wanted to stay in his good books, you'd better be there too.

There was just one problem. Ms. Lawson had scheduled our first weekend rehearsal for tomorrow morning. Until now, I hadn't really thought about which one of those must-attend events I was going to miss.

chapter nine

Dad usually tried to let Mom sleep in on Saturday mornings. He and I had got into the habit of quietly eating breakfast together and then heading out of the house without disturbing her.

As usual, we didn't say much to each other as we munched our toast, and Dad finished his coffee. He was on his way to his pickup-hoops game. Dad played a couple of times a week with the same bunch of forty-something guys. They had all played a little in high school and still acted as though they were aiming for the NBA. Most of them could barely get up and down the court twice in a row. I had spent many Saturday mornings in the gym watching Dad and his buddies. Once I was big enough to avoid being steamrolled, I joined in their games. But I had stopped playing with Dad and his friends as basketball at school got more and more serious. I couldn't afford to get injured now. And besides, I was getting too fast for the old guys.

"Let's go, Kyle," Dad said as he grabbed his gym bag and water bottle.

It was now routine for Dad to drop me off at Sainsbury before he went to his pickup game. It only took a few minutes to reach the high school. "How was Coach last night?" Dad asked, already knowing the answer.

"He wasn't happy," I replied.

"Well, he couldn't have been too upset with how you played," Dad said. "I thought you guarded Eric really well. And Stillman should have got you the ball on that last play."

I had to agree with Dad. He and I nearly always saw the game the same way—probably because he was my father. But I didn't tell him that Coach had actually been mad at me—not Stillman—after the game. No sense getting Dad worked up about anything. Saturday was his time to relax.

"Thanks for the ride," I said, hopping out in the Sainsbury parking lot.

"Have a good practice," Dad said before pulling away. He was always in a good mood on Saturday mornings. It was the one day he didn't have to worry about chasing down stories for the *Bulletin*. He could just play basketball. Sometimes I thought he loved basketball even more than I did.

As I walked toward the gym, I saw Ms. Lawson getting out of her silver Honda Civic. She was carrying a box full of costume accessories and small props, and she seemed in danger of dumping them all over the parking lot. I grabbed her car door and helped steady the load.

"Thank you, Kyle." She smiled. "It's nice to see you here so early this morning."

I nodded. I didn't know how to tell Ms. Lawson that I wasn't there for rehearsal. I didn't say anything as I walked with her into the theater, lugging the large box of hats, scarves, gloves and other bits and pieces.

Ms. Lawson went straight into the prop room behind the stage. "Kyle, have you seen these?" she called out. "They're absolutely gorgeous!"

I stuck my head into the prop room, where the painted sets for *Oliver!* were lined up against the wall. They had been created on a series of colorful six-by-ten-foot backdrops. Ms. Lawson was right. They were beautiful. The kids who had worked on the sets had done a fantastic job. One backdrop depicted Fagin's underworld hideout. Another was a perfect likeness of a pub. My favorite was the London street scene where Dodger—me—would instruct young Oliver in the fine art of pickpocketing.

"They're awesome," I acknowledged. "Kind of gets you pumped up for the show."

Ms. Lawson smiled. "No kidding," she said. "But we've still got some serious work to do."

There was half an hour until the rehearsal started. "I'm just going to Starbucks to pick up a latte," Ms. Lawson said cheerily. "Can I get you anything, Kyle?"

I shook my head. As Ms. Lawson headed back to the parking lot, I ducked back outside and made my way to the gym. Luckily, I didn't run into anybody else from the cast.

Unfortunately, the side trip to the theater had thrown me off-schedule. Even though the Saturday shootaround was "optional," I noticed Coach Williams glance at me and then again at his watch as I came through the gym doors. By now it was

9:05 AM, and everybody else on the team was already in the gym, chatting, bouncing balls and taking the occasional shot.

"Nice to see you, *Dodger*," an unmistakable voice called from the far end of the gym. A few of the other boys snickered at Ben Stillman's crack. "How come you're late? Spend the night with *Fag*-in?"

I felt my face growing red and my ears tingling. Stillman was obviously referring to Lukas Connor. It wasn't the first time that the idiot had made a stupid remark about Lukas being gay.

I marched toward Stillman, who was at the far free-throw line, standing with the ball on his hip. "What exactly is your problem?" I said, looking directly into his black eyes.

"Just you," Stillman replied, an irritating smirk forming at one corner of his mouth. "I thought you were supposed to be a basketball player, not one of the funny boys of the drama department."

Again, Stillman's remarks drew a few snickers. I was sure Coach Williams could hear what was going on. Why didn't he step in and stop this jerk?

"You're a loser, Stillman," I said, moving toward him. "And if you spent as much time worrying about your free throws as you do worrying about other people's business, we would have won that game last night."

"Check the score sheet," Stillman shot back.

"My mom could score twenty-one too, if every play was run for her," I replied. "And she wouldn't have messed up that last play, either."

Now it was Stillman's face that went red. He lunged toward me, shoving his right arm into my shoulder. The force knocked me back a step, but it didn't really hurt.

"Just like I thought, Evans," Stillman seethed. "You're just as soft as your little buddies in the theater."

That was enough for me. I stepped up to Stillman and swung with my right fist. The blow wasn't as hard as I could hit, but it was close. My fist glanced off the side of Stillman's right ear. He covered the area with his palm, bending forward in pain.

"Evans!" Coach Williams yelled. "What the heck are you doing!" Oh great, *now* he steps in!

"Both you guys. In my office. Right now," the coach barked. "The rest of you scrimmage while I straighten this out."

Less than two minutes later, Stillman and I sat side by side in wooden chairs, facing the coach across his desk. Coach Williams cleared his throat and leaned back in his chair.

"I don't know what this is all about...," he began.

"It's Evans, Coach," Stillman replied. "He comes in late and then he just goes off on me."

I couldn't believe my ears. I went off on him? He should write fiction.

"Coach, he was riding me, like he always does," I said. "I'm tired of his crap.

He's got a problem with me. But maybe he should just concentrate on his own game."

Coach Williams looked at me carefully, then at Stillman, and then back at me. Without even looking at Ben, he said, "Stillman, get back out there. I want to talk to Evans for a few minutes."

The door closed behind Stillman. Coach Williams sighed.

"Kyle, I have big hopes for you as a basketball player," he said. I could almost hear the "but" coming in the next sentence before he said it.

"But I'm worried that you're letting this drama thing get in the way of your concentration, both on the court and off. This is the second time in less than two weeks that you've been late to practice. And now I see you punching Stillman. I'm not sure what's gotten into you."

I couldn't believe what I was hearing. What's gotten into *me*? Had the coach seen anything that had gone on out there? Had he ever taken a good look at what

Ben Stillman was really like? And what did the play have to do with anything? I had been late for one real practice and that happened before I had even thought about trying out for *Oliver!*

All I could manage out loud was, "Sorry, Coach."

"I want you to do something—for me and for yourself," the coach said. "I want you to go home after this practice, and use the rest of the weekend to decide whether you really want to play basketball for Sainsbury. Think about whether you can commit one hundred percent to it."

"Okay, Coach," I replied.

My face burned as I left his office. For the rest of the shootaround, I simply went through the motions, avoiding Stillman whenever I could and never looking the coach directly in the eye. I usually loved nothing better than shooting hoops with my friends on a Saturday morning. On this particular Saturday I no longer wanted to be there.

It was just after 11:00 AM by the time I returned to the Sainsbury theater. Kids were clustered together in several small groups, running through their lines. Ms. Lawson was moving between them, making suggestions. I had been in the theater only a few seconds when she noticed me.

"Kyle, can I speak to you a minute?" she said. The usual friendly singsong tone in her voice was missing. I gulped.

"Where have you been for the last two hours?" she asked. "I know you were here earlier. But then we called your name for group reading and you were gone."

"I had basketball shootaround," I replied sheepishly. "It's every Saturday. Coach expects us to be there."

"And you can't be two places at once. I understand, but you did tell me there wouldn't be any conflicts," Ms. Lawson said. The way she spoke didn't sound like she understood at all. "I'll talk to Coach Williams about it," she continued with a sigh. "Maybe there's a way we can compromise here—each get you for an hour on Saturday morning or something like that."

I nodded. It sounded like a reasonable solution. But somehow, I didn't think Coach Williams was going to see it that way.

chapter ten

By Monday morning, I was a little bit calmer about basketball. Mom and Dad had figured out that something was bothering me. We hashed it out over dinner on Sunday night. Neither of them gave me an instant solution to my problems. Mom told me to "try to ignore" Ben Stillman. Dad suggested I have a "heart-to-heart" with Coach Williams. But at least I had been able to talk to somebody about it.

As usual, I headed to school for Monday's 7:30 AM practice. I wasn't about to be late. We had an away game against Echo Valley the following Friday. I knew Coach would be even more intense during practice this week. After losing our opener, we couldn't afford any more slippage.

As I reached the Sainsbury parking lot, I noticed a white police cruiser parked directly in front of the school's main doors. That was weird. What were the cops doing there on a Monday morning? There was no time to check it out, though, not if I wanted to be on time for practice.

I had been stewing about this practice after my clashes with Ben Stillman and Coach Williams, but the session was routine. In fact, we spent much of the time scrimmaging. Stillman and I actually hooked up for a couple of slick passing plays between the high and low post. The entire team ran crisply through the one-hour session. I could tell Coach was pleased. "Evans, Stillman—now that's more like it!" He smiled at us as we left the floor. Stillman and I didn't talk or make any eye contact off the court or in the locker room after practice. That suited me just fine.

My first class was math, which made Monday mornings even more of a drag than they already were. I worked hard enough to maintain a C-plus average in math. Anything lower than a C meant no extracurricular activities. Translation: No basketball. No theater. So, although I detested math, I understood how important it was to survive it.

On my way to Mr. Riley's room, I spotted Lukas Connor. He was standing outside the theater doors with Brad Schmidt and Ollie Jacobs. "Kyle!" Luke motioned me over, his voice high and excited. "You're not going to believe this. It's all ruined. Everything."

"What are you talking about?" I asked.

"The sets for the play," Luke replied. "All those backdrops. Somebody trashed all of them. Check it out."

Luke motioned toward the theater door, which was open. I stepped inside and stared at the stage, where several painted backdrops lay strewn across the wooden floor. All those scenes that the drama kids had spent hours crafting on Friday night were now lying in tatters. Whoever had done this had punched holes through the backdrops and ripped the London street scene completely in half. The pub backdrop had huge ragged scratches across it. But that wasn't the worst of it.

Across the backdrop that represented Fagin's hideout were huge letters in black paint. I couldn't believe what I was reading: *Fag-in's Place*.

I turned to look at Lukas. "Who would do something like this?" I said.

"Who knows?" Luke replied, shaking his head slowly. "I do know the cops were here checking it out this morning."

That explained the police cruiser I had seen at the school on my way to practice.

But what was the point of wrecking all this stuff?

"Hello, boys." Ms. Lawson's greeting interrupted my thoughts. I turned and glanced at her. Her usual chipper attitude was muted this morning. Instead of a wide warm smile, the edges of her mouth dipped downward. Her brow was wrinkled. She looked as though she hadn't slept well last night.

"Pretty upsetting, isn't it?" she said, her shoulders slumping. "I got here first thing this morning to find those scenes lying there like that. Now we'll have to start all over again. Can I count on you boys to help over the next few mornings?"

Luke, Brad and Ollie all nodded. "I'd like to," I pitched in, "but I've got practice in the mornings." I felt guilty, like somehow I wasn't pulling my weight or helping Ms. Lawson when she really needed it. Double-guilty, that is, since I had ducked out of Saturday morning's rehearsal without telling her first.

"That's okay, Kyle," Ms. Lawson reassured me. "I know you've got a crazy schedule."

Lukas and I began walking toward our first class of the day. He had a chemistry lab right beside my early-morning math block. "I just need to get a book from my locker," he said. "Wait up."

I stood a few feet behind Luke as he fumbled with the combination lock. The locker door sprang open, and a terrible smell filled the hallway. Inside the locker sat a plastic bag full of something—something brown. On it was taped a note which read *To the Sainsbury Drama QUEEN*.

I was shocked. First, the smell coming from the plastic bag was almost enough to gag us. But as bad as that was, the note was even worse.

I looked at Luke's face. Tears were welling up in his eyes. His skin seemed even paler than usual. He was trembling. "What the hell?" he said, slamming the locker door shut. "It's dog crap," he said with disgust. "Somebody put dog crap in my locker. What the hell?"

"You've got to go to the office," I said. "You've got to report this."

I felt horrible for Lukas. I'd never really realized that people had such a problem with him. And I didn't really understand it. What did it matter if he was different? Who was he hurting?

"First I'm going to get rid of it," Luke said, opening his locker and reaching in for the bag.

"Better not," I warned. "You should show it to somebody first. It's evidence. So is the note. Just lock it all up."

Lukas and I walked to the main office. Mrs. Marsh, the school secretary, looked up as we entered. "What are you boys doing out of class?" she asked suspiciously.

"Sorry," Luke said. "But we need to see Mr. Jensen. It's urgent."

As Lukas and I explained to the Sainsbury principal what had happened, Mr. Jensen's brow furrowed above his wire-rimmed glasses.

"I'm sorry this happened to you, Lukas," he said quietly. "The school has zero tolerance for this sort of thing. Whoever did this will be dealt with severely, I can promise you that. You did the right thing coming to me." He sighed. "It's been a bad morning here at Sainsbury. I know you boys are in the cast for *Oliver!* Did you see what happened to the sets?"

Luke and I looked at each other and nodded. After what we had discovered in his locker, we had almost forgotten about the sets. What was going on at this school, anyway?

After the principal had inspected Luke's locker in person, he turned to us. "I am going to call the police back and tell them about this incident too," he said. "In the meantime, you boys should get to class.

Try to have a good day, if you can. I'll take care of this mess."

Lukas smiled weakly. "I'll catch you later," he said, his slender shoulders rolling forward as he walked toward the chemistry room.

"Yeah, later," I said. "Hey, Luke, I'm sorry, man."

I watched him open the door to the lab and walk inside. I felt better for having told him I was sorry. But why was I really apologizing?

The principal had provided me with a note explaining to Mr. Riley why I was late for math. I took my spot at the back of the classroom and pulled out my workbook. That was it as far as math went for me that morning, though. All kinds of thoughts were invading my brain.

I had been shocked to see the vandalism of Luke's locker, but was the note on that bag really so stunning? If I was honest with myself I'd have to say no.

I knew how guys in this school, especially the jock crowd, talked and joked about kids like Lukas. I had heard all the terms—gay, homo, fairy, queer, queen, fag. I had even used them once or twice myself.

But until this morning, I hadn't thought about what those words actually meant or how hurtful they could be. I was ashamed of myself for not realizing that before. Luke was a good kid. He didn't deserve this. At the front of the room, Mr. Riley droned on and on. I heard none of it.

I managed to track Luke down in the cafeteria at lunchtime. He was sitting with Brad and Ollie. "You got a minute?" I asked.

"Sure," Lukas said. "What's up?"

"Can I talk to you outside for a second?"

Luke looked puzzled. We walked out the cafeteria door and down the steps into the courtyard. There was an empty bench at the far end. Nobody else was around.

"Pretty messed up morning, huh?" Luke said.

"Yeah, that's kind of what I wanted to talk to you about," I said. "I was thinking about that note in your locker and what was painted on that one set in the theater. It's not right. I mean, who cares if you're gay?"

The words had just tumbled out of me. It wasn't exactly the way I had planned to say it, but at least now it was out there. I wanted to let Lukas know that I disagreed with people who called him names and made fun of him just because he was gay. I wanted to let him know I was on his side.

Lukas just sat there on the bench with a stunned expression on his face. "I'm not sure what to say to that," he mumbled.

"What I'm trying to tell you is, I don't care if you're gay," I said. "I think the stuff in that note was really stupid."

Luke was now shaking his head rapidly. He drew a deep breath. His voice got louder as he spoke. "You know what, Kyle?

I expect this from some of the morons on the basketball or football teams, but not from you. I thought you were my friend, but I see you're just like everybody else in this stupid school."

"Luke, I..."

"I gotta go," Lukas said, turning away and running up the stairs. He disappeared quickly through the glass doors and down the hallway.

Things had not gone the way I had planned. I had wanted to let Luke know that I supported him. But it obviously hadn't made him feel any better. In fact, I was pretty sure I'd just made things a whole lot worse.

chapter eleven

I found it really difficult to get to sleep
that night. So much was running through
my mind. I felt horrible about the way
things had gone with Lukas. I was still
shaken over the vandalism to his locker
and to the *Oliver!* sets. And I was worried about my place on the basketball
team. How was I going to deal with Ben
Stillman? And was Coach Williams going

to be on my case for the rest of my high-school life?

It was close to midnight. My reading light was still on. I was absentmindedly thumbing through the pages of *Slam* magazine when Dad stuck his head into my room. "Kyle," he said. "You should be asleep, guy. You've got practice early tomorrow."

"I know," I said. "I was just thinking."

"About what?"

"Nothing, really," I said. "Well, a lot, actually. Well, it's hard to explain..."

Dad had that look on his face—his eyebrows arched and his jaw clenched tightly—that he gets whenever he is concerned about me. He sat down on the far end of my bed. "What's going on?" he said.

It came out in a rush. All the stuff about the vandalism and Lukas. How I had tried to talk to him afterward. How Lukas was now pissed at me, like just about everybody else seemed to be.

"I can see why all that would leave you thinking," Dad said. "You guys had quite a day."

He took a deep breath and patted my feet before resuming. "You know, Kyle, you shouldn't worry too much. You and Lukas will work things out. But you've probably learned something valuable here about homophobia."

Homophobia? I hadn't really thought about it clearly until now, but I knew he was right. That's exactly what this was—the fear or hatred of gay people.

Dad had written a series of prize-winning articles for the *Bulletin* last year about homophobia and its effects on the gay community in our city. I remembered reading them and wondering what it must feel like to be persecuted and excluded, sometimes even within your own family.

"What's going on at your school is exactly the sort of thing I was writing about," Dad said. "It's something that is fed by ignorance. And it almost always results in somebody getting hurt."

I gulped. I had seen the hurt in Luke's eyes after he opened his locker this morning and again when he and I had spoken in the courtyard. I had been confused by his reaction. I still wasn't sure if he was gay or not. But I was certain it had been a miserable day for him.

"I feel bad about it," I said. "I mean, I don't even know if Luke is gay..."

"Does it matter?" Dad said.

I shook my head. It shouldn't matter, I thought. But had I let it matter over the last few years? Had I stopped hanging around with Lukas because I thought he was "different"? And because I didn't want to be seen as "different" too?

At lunch hour the next day, I tracked down Jenna, who was eating with a bunch of kids from the musical. "Hey, Kyle." She smiled sweetly, grabbing my hand. "I didn't see much of you yesterday."

"Nah, I got tied up," I said. "I mean, I had something on my mind. Got some time to talk about it?"

She looked concerned. "Sure," she said. "Let's go for a walk."

Jenna and I circled the school grounds slowly. She bit into a green apple she had packed for lunch. "What's going on, Kyle?" she said, stopping and looking me directly in the eyes.

"It's Luke," I said. "I guess you heard what happened to his locker."

Jenna nodded. "That was rough," she said. "I felt so bad for him. He was pretty shaken up by it."

"Is Luke gay?" I just blurted it out. "I mean, I told him yesterday that I was sorry kids were hassling him because he is. But he freaked out and took off. Now I don't know what to think."

Jenna was silent.

"All the guys are always calling him names," I continued. "And he is sort of on the feminine side. I guess I just thought..."

"Kyle, you've known him for years," Jenna interrupted. "If it mattered so much to you, why didn't you just ask him?"

Good question. Seemed pretty simple in hindsight. But maybe I hadn't wanted to know the answer. Maybe it had been easier just to ignore him. I hadn't bullied or teased Lukas like Ben Stillman and his buddies had, but I had never stepped up to stop it, either. And for the past five years I hadn't been a very good friend to Luke at all.

Ms. Lawson assembled the entire cast and crew in the front two rows of the theater before Tuesday afternoon's rehearsal.

"Okay, kids," she said. "By now, everybody knows what happened to our sets. We've got a lot of work to do to put things back together. We got a good start on it this morning. Let's run through our scenes now. Hopefully, the new backdrops will be ready by Monday.

"In the meantime, I want to let you know that the police have the security tapes from the theater and are going over them now. So whoever trashed the sets will hopefully be caught."

I was happy to hear that. I wondered what kind of morons would just destroy something for no reason.

Lukas and I walked home together after the rehearsal. We were silent for the first block. Then I worked up the nerve to talk about what I had been worrying about.

"Luke, man, I'm sorry for just assuming you were gay," I finally said.

Lukas stopped walking and stared at me. "It's nobody's business if I'm gay, straight or bi-sexual," he said. "What difference does it make?"

"So *are* you, or not?" I had to ask the question.

Lukas shut his eyes for a second. He sucked in a big gulp of air, then exhaled slowly. He was looking down at the ground.

"I don't know—okay?" he said, his voice growing sharp. "I just don't know. I realize everybody wants to put a label on me, but it's not that easy. Sometimes I think I am, and other times it's really confusing. It's easier just not to think too much about it."

Luke's voice was now breaking and he was near tears. "Look," he said, his blue eyes now meeting mine directly. "If even *I'm* not sure whether I'm gay, how come so many other people seem to be? And what possible difference does it make to anybody in this school? What difference does it make to you, Kyle? I'm still me. Same guy I've been all along."

I was silent. It shouldn't make any difference, but somehow I had let it.

"I guess what bugs me a lot more than anybody calling me names is that you and I haven't hung out for a few years," Luke continued. "I never really understood what that was all about and I was afraid to ask you. I thought it was mostly about me not liking sports. But if it was *really* because of this? I mean, that's pretty lame."

He was right. I knew it. I had no defense.

"I don't think I ever consciously chose not to hang out with you because of that," I said. "But I guess in the back of my mind it was there...and maybe I never tried out for theater before because I didn't think it was what 'real' guys did."

Luke laughed bitterly. "I feel sorry for you, man," he said. "You're a talented actor and singer and you let something like what other people think stop you?"

As Luke spoke, I realized that's exactly what I had done. And I also realized that Luke—all five-foot-nothing and 120 pounds of him—had been strong enough to go after his dreams no matter what anybody else thought.

"What can I say?" I smiled weakly at Lukas. "I'm an idiot?"

Luke took my surrender graciously. "Aren't all jocks idiots?" He winked. "I mean, I just assumed..."

I had to laugh at his line. Luke had nailed it—and me—big time.

chapter twelve

I spent a lot of time that night thinking about what Luke and I had talked about and how closed-minded I had been. I had missed out on a great friendship, but it looked like he was willing to give me another chance. I'd definitely missed out on developing whatever talent I had on stage. I hoped it wasn't too late.

I knew all the things Luke had said about me were true. And it had taken being

part of *Oliver!* for me to realize that basketball and theater actually had some things
in common. In both cases, the people
involved were passionate and deeply committed to doing their best. They worked as
a team and looked out for each other. They
weren't really two different worlds at all.

I also couldn't help but think about all
the times my basketball teammates and I
had used the words *gay* and *fag* and *queer*.
We hadn't really meant that stuff to be
hateful—I hadn't, anyway—but that's what it
was.

My mind flashed back to when I'd had
the run-in with Ben Stillman and Coach
Williams at the gym on Saturday. What was
it that Stillman had said to me when I first
came in the door for the shootaround?
"Spend the night with Fag-in?"

I bolted upright in bed, shaking. The
graffiti on one of the backdrops that had
been vandalized had contained the same
stupid play on words: *Fag-in.* Could Stillman
be responsible for the vandalism to the sets?

And had he been responsible for putting the dog crap in Luke's locker too?

I didn't want to believe that, even though I couldn't stand the guy. But the more I thought about it, the more it made sense. Stillman had been making fun of Lukas ever since I could remember. And he had seemed to have a hate-on for *Oliver!* since the day we saw the audition poster in the hallway. I didn't have any hard evidence, but the possibility that Stillman was somehow involved ran through my head as I finally drifted off to sleep.

I arrived at school Wednesday morning to once again discover a police cruiser parked in the circular driveway. This certainly was shaping up to be an eventful week at Sainsbury.

We were only halfway through basketball practice when two uniformed officers marched through the double doors of the gym. They motioned from the sidelines for Coach Williams to come over and speak with them. After a minute or so of conversation with the police, Coach blew his whistle. "I'm cutting practice early today," he said quietly, his face suddenly pale. "You guys can all hit the showers."

We began to disperse, wondering what was going on. "Armstrong, Flatley, I need to see you over here," Coach said.

I glanced over at Joey Armstrong and Kurt Flatley. Each had a pained expression on his face, as if coming over to speak with the coach was the most difficult thing in the world. As I walked into the locker room, I saw the two policemen talking to the coach and the two boys.

"Wonder what's happening out there?" Sammy asked the question we had all been thinking.

"No idea," said Pete Freeman. "If the cops should be after anybody on this team it should be me. I lead the league in steals."

We all groaned at his bad joke, but it didn't do much to lighten the mood in the locker room. We showered and dressed in relative quiet. Each of us was feeling concerned and confused about why the police had come to the gym. And we knew it had to be something pretty serious for the coach to cut practice in half.

It was midmorning when the announcement came over the school loudspeakers during history class. "May I have everyone's attention for a minute?" The deep voice belonged to Mr. Jensen.

"A special assembly will be held at eleven-fifty-five this morning in the gymnasium," he continued. "All students and staff are to attend."

An hour later, a buzz rippled through the hallways as over eight hundred Sainsbury students made their way toward the gym, the only place large enough to hold the entire student body. Teachers lined us up by class, and we sat in rows on the same shiny hardwood floor where I had sweated through so many basketball practices.

"Good morning, students," the principal said as he stepped to the mike. "Today's assembly concerns something very serious.

I'll keep it brief, so we can all continue with our lunch hour.

"As you might have noticed, the police were here again this morning," he continued. "They have reviewed the security videotape from the theater and identified two of the students responsible for the damage to the sets for the school musical. Those students have been suspended."

A murmur rolled across the gym floor. Everybody looked around, trying to spot the guilty students.

"The officers saw a third figure on the security tape, but they haven't yet been able to determine who it was," the principal said. "Thus far, the two students who have admitted to taking part in the vandalism have refused to implicate that third person.

"I am making an appeal to the student body. If you know who this third person is, please come forward. Your identity will be kept confidential. Of course, if that person wants to come forward, that would be even better."

A few kids in the gym chuckled quietly. Nobody stepped forward. Big surprise.

"I want to remind everybody that acts of hatred and vandalism are not tolerated here at Sainsbury," the principal said. "It's not who we are. That's all."

My head was reeling. It was obvious now that Joey Armstrong and Kurt Flatley had been responsible for the damage to the play backdrops. But they hadn't acted alone. Those two guys were tight with Ben Stillman. I pieced together all the anti-gay comments Stillman had made during the past few weeks. He *had* to be the third person involved. And I was pretty sure the three of them had trashed Luke's locker too.

My first instinct was to march straight up to Principal Jensen and tell him what I knew. Or thought I knew. I didn't have any actual proof, but there were certainly plenty of signs pointing to Stillman.

My thoughts were interrupted by Coach Williams's stern voice. He had grabbed the microphone at the front of the gym. "Could I just get your attention, please?" he said. "I would like all the senior varsity basketball players to meet in the locker room for a few minutes. Thank you."

Sammy fell in behind me as I made my way to the locker room. "What's up?" I asked. Sammy just looked at me and shrugged his shoulders.

The rest of the team was inside by the time Sammy and I got there, yet the locker room was eerily quiet. Coach Williams occupied his usual spot in the middle of the room. He wore a somber look and heaved a large sigh as he began to address the group.

"Fellas, I hate to say this," Coach said as he looked around the locker room. "I had to suspend two members of our team today. Joey Armstrong and Kurt Flatley have admitted to wrecking the drama sets last Saturday. I don't have to tell you how disappointed I am over that news. It's not what I expect from any of you."

We all looked at the floor, at the walls, anywhere but into the eyes of our disappointed coach.

"As Principal Jensen said, there was a third person in the videotapes," Coach continued. "If anyone else from this team was involved, I'd like him to step forward right now."

Silence. Nobody made a move. I glanced over at Stillman. His eyes were fixed on the gray tile floor of the locker room. But I could clearly see his face. It carried an expression that I had never seen on him before: a cross between fear and nausea.

"Okay, then," Coach said, looking somewhat relieved. "We'll practice tomorrow, as usual. Let's put this behind us and get ready for Friday, all right?"

The coach extended his right hand into the middle of the room. The rest of us followed suit, putting our right hands on top of his. "One, two, three—Eagles!" we yelled. The cheer had always made me feel good before a game or after a practice, but right now it seemed out of place.

chapter thirteen

By the time our rehearsal for *Oliver!* was over that afternoon, I knew I had to share my suspicions with somebody. The third person in that security video had to be Ben Stillman. It all fit together perfectly.

But what could I do? I had no hard evidence. And if Stillman was booted off the team it might not completely ruin our basketball season, but it would come close. Joey Armstrong and Kurt Flatley may have been second-stringers but they had still been tough, dependable players. Now they were gone. If I ratted on Stillman, one of our key starters would be gone. And more than likely our chances of winning the regional title would be history too.

I knew telling someone my suspicions was probably the right thing to do. But how would that look to the rest of my teammates? They knew Ben and I had been rivals for the last few years. They'd probably just think that I was ratting him out so that I could become the star of the Sainsbury show. And if I was being totally honest, I had to admit that at least a small part of me thought it would be pretty cool to have Stillman out of the way.

I must have been unusually quiet on the walk home because Lukas noticed after just a few minutes. "What's the matter?" he asked.

"I've just got something on my mind."

"Me too," Lukas replied.

"Oh yeah?"

"I just don't get it," Lukas said. "I mean, what's wrong with people in this school?"

"What do you mean?"

"Well, why would anybody do something like that to my locker?"

That was a tough one. There was no good answer. I just shook my head.

"I don't know..."

"Well, neither do I, but it sucks," Lukas said. "Ever since about sixth grade, I've been hearing it. This is just more obvious than it's ever been before."

"Hearing what?" I said.

"Things about me being gay, being queer," Lukas said. "I mean, why does it matter to people so much?"

Lukas fixed his gaze on me. I knew he wanted answers, but I didn't have any—none that made sense, anyway.

I thought about the articles my dad had written last year. "I guess a lot of people are afraid of anything or anybody that's different," I said.

"Afraid...of what? That's just so—"

I interrupted him in mid-sentence. "Luke, look, I'm not saying it's right, but you asked, so I'm telling you. I think it does have a lot to do with how you look and act. You're not a jock, you like theater, you dress different and you're kind of, uh, soft-spoken. A lot of guys think that's weird."

Luke laughed bitterly. "Whatever, Kyle," he said. "I know I'm a little different, but what's wrong with that? Do I have to act like all the rest of you guys—like my whole life revolves around sports and hunting and monster truck shows?"

This time I laughed nervously. But what Luke was saying made a lot of sense. It also made me feel guilty.

"I was thinking about what you said about not wanting to be in theater because you didn't think it was what 'real' guys did," he added. "But what do you think pro wrestling is? Or lots of other pro sports, for that matter? They're all about drama and entertainment, just like our little Sainsbury production, you know, if not more."

That idea stopped me for a second. I was just mulling it over when Luke hit me again.

"Besides," he said, "don't people realize there are gay athletes out there? God, Kyle, something like ten percent of the population is gay. So there's a good chance that somebody on your basketball team is."

I had heard the statistics too. And just last year I had read a story about John Amaechi, a long time NBA player who had written a book about his career as a gay pro athlete. There were no doubt plenty of professional and amateur athletes who hid their lifestyles because they might be misunderstood or harassed, just like Lukas had been. All those locker room jokes I had heard and even participated in now seemed pretty juvenile. And in contrast to me and some of my friends, Luke Connor seemed downright mature.

I realized now I had been guilty of a lot of things. Of shunning Luke because he was different, but also of buying into the notion that being gay was something to be ashamed of. What if I had been born gay? How would I have wanted to be treated? I already knew the answer to that.

chapter fourteen

The main thing that kept me awake that night wasn't my guilt about Luke. It was the question of what, exactly, I should do with my suspicions about Ben Stillman.

If I went to Coach Williams, I didn't know how he would react. Probably not well. He had already lost two players this week. Losing his leading scorer and "meal ticket" might just send him over the edge.

If I spoke to my parents about it, it could get really complicated. They'd probably want to go talk to Principal Jensen right away. And although I trusted Dad, I didn't want him turning it into a human-interest column in the Sunday *Bulletin*.

Then it hit me. I could turn over the information to Lukas. He was the one who had been most affected. He could decide how to proceed.

The next morning, I got up good and early and waited on the corner of Albion and Bank for Lukas to show. At about 7:45 AM he appeared, wearing his usual dress slacks and shiny black shoes with a white argyle sweater. Luke obviously wasn't about to change his style just to fit in.

"Hey, Kyle," he said, looking surprised. "Were you waiting for me?"

"Yeah," I said. "I need to tell you something."

A flash of concern crossed Lukas's face. "Sounds serious," he said.

"It is," I replied. I launched headlong into my suspicions about Ben Stillman. How the things he had said to me were so similar to the messages that had been scrawled on both the play props and on the note in Luke's locker. How Stillman was good friends with Joey Armstrong and Kurt Flatley. How Stillman was a huge jerk who was completely capable of doing stupid and hateful things.

"Well," I said, looking at Lukas. "What do you want to do about it?"

"Nothing," Luke said flatly.

"Nothing? What do you mean nothing? Don't you want to nail this guy?"

Luke paused and heaved a sigh. "Kyle, I already knew it was Stillman," he said slowly. "When the police showed me the videotape of the kids in the theater, I saw the letters *ley* on the arm of the hoodie that the third kid was wearing. I know Stillman has a Hurley hoodie just like that. And the kid in the video was pretty big. You don't have to be James Bond to figure it out. The cops are pretty sure the same kids who wrecked the sets also did that stuff to my locker. Makes sense to me too."

I was confused. Lukas already knew it was Stillman? Why hadn't he said something? Why hadn't he gone to the principal or to the cops? If I had seen the tapes I would have recognized Stillman's jacket too.

"So, why don't you tell somebody?" I said.

"I thought about it," Lukas replied quietly. "But what's the point? Stillman is a huge basketball star, isn't he? So if I turned him in, it would just hurt the school's chances. It would hurt kids like you who have worked hard for years. Stillman and his buddies would be pissed at me. I'd have to watch my back. And do you think anything would really change because of it?"

I shook my head. Luke was right. Stillman wasn't the kind of kid to learn a lesson from something like this, even if it was obvious enough to hit him square between the eyes. Luke was smart enough to know that. He was also considerate enough to realize how much losing Stillman would hurt our team's chances this year. But it wasn't right.

"This is messed up," I said. "Stillman does something like this, gets away with it and still gets to play basketball."

Lukas shook his head. "I know, it's not perfect. But I've thought about it. I don't want to be the one who brings the Eagles down. And I'm banking on the odds that, one day, Ben Stillman is going to run into somebody bigger and more ignorant than he is."

I laughed. "Somebody like that might be tough to find."

Lukas chuckled. "I've gotta go," he said. "I'm working with Ms. Lawson on my lines this morning."

"All right, man. Later," I said, reaching out to shake his hand.

Luke smiled. "You comfortable with this?" he said as our palms met. "Or do you think maybe we should wait until the second date?"

I laughed out loud. I was really happy that Luke wasn't holding a grudge. He was a pretty tolerant guy. Way more tolerant than a lot of people.

"Later," he said, heading off toward the theater.

While Luke and I had been talking and walking through the parking lot, I hadn't noticed the tall, solitary figure hanging about half a block behind us.

"Hey, Evans, wait up!"

The deep voice calling my name through the crisp autumn air caught me by surprise. I spun around.

"I have to talk to you."

I turned and faced Ben Stillman, who by now was just a few feet away. His usual sneering smile was missing. He looked downright worried.

"I saw you talking to that Connor kid," Stillman said slowly. "What's up?"

"What do you mean?" I said.

"I mean, what were you two talking about?"

"I've known Luke for years," I shot back. "Since when do I have to tell you what I'm talking to a friend about?"

"Don't screw with me," Stillman seethed. "If you two are planning to tell Coach what I did, I'd think twice if I were you."

"Tell him what?" I replied. "Is there something bothering your conscience, Stillman? If you have one, that is?"

Stillman jumped toward me, putting his face just inches in front of mine. He was close enough that I could feel his anger. I couldn't help but notice he was wearing the brown Hurley hoodie that had played a starring role in the security video. He really wasn't very bright.

"Think about it," Stillman snarled. "If you guys turn me in, there goes the basketball season."

"Turn you in?" I said. "You're such a dork, Stillman. I had no proof that you even did anything until now. You just confessed."

A pained expression crossed Ben Stillman's face. "I need a scholarship," he growled. "Nobody's going to mess with that. Nobody. Especially not that little drama queen. Or you."

I'd heard enough. My head grew hot and my temper surged out of control.

"You don't even know Lukas," I yelled. "So just shut up about him."

Stillman leaned forward again, his tone menacing. "Just make sure he doesn't rat me out."

"Don't worry," I said. "Lukas has proof you messed with the sets and that you probably trashed his locker too. But he isn't going to turn you in."

"What?" Stillman said.

"Luke knows that if you're stupid enough to do something like that, you have bigger problems. No suspension is going to fix them. He doesn't want to mess things up for the basketball team. He's a pretty cool kid...a lot cooler than you."

Stillman was silent. I left him standing there, alone in the parking lot, wearing his Hurley hoodie and a stunned expression.

The more I thought about the parking lot confrontation with Stillman, the more I admired Lukas's decision not to turn him in. Even though he had been bullied by Stillman and his buddies for years, Luke didn't seem to have a huge appetite for revenge. Luke's maturity had surprised me, but it had absolutely floored Ben Stillman.

Yet I also couldn't help but feel that Stillman was being rewarded for acting like an idiot. Seeing him escape punishment for what he had done was driving me crazy.

I needed to talk to somebody about the situation. Somebody who had no stake in the basketball team. Somebody who was a good listener. I knew just the person. Jenna.

I found her at lunchtime. Once again, she was eating in the cafeteria with kids from the drama group. Their table was bubbling over with excitement about *Oliver!* Performances were now less than a month away. Already the cast was becoming a tight group even though we'd been rehearsing for less than three weeks. Each of us looked forward to the first time we'd be able to put everything together on stage for an actual audience.

"You nervous, Kyle?" asked Ollie Jacobs. "I mean, you've got to sing by yourself in front of so many people."

"Don't remind me," I groaned. "I think I feel a wicked sore throat coming on."

Jenna chuckled. "You'll do great, Kyle," she said. "I've been listening to you in rehearsals. You're awesome."

I blushed as the rest of the kids at the table looked my way. Nobody else said anything. I wondered if they thought I was even half as good as Jenna did.

"Can I talk to you alone?" I asked.

"Sure," she said.

We again strolled the school grounds. A light autumn rain was falling, which meant almost everyone else was inside. "I'm wondering what to do about this situation," I said.

"What situation?" Jenna replied.

"I know who the third guy is on that videotape. The one who helped wreck the *Oliver!* scenes and trash Luke's locker."

Jenna arched her eyebrows in surprise. "Who is it?" she said.

"It's Ben Stillman. I'm sure of it."

"Stillman? Are you serious?"

"Totally," I said. "And part of me wants to tell somebody. But another part wants to keep it quiet. It would obviously hurt our team if he got suspended, even though he definitely deserves it."

Jenna was thinking it over.

"I'd say you don't have any choice," she said finally. "This isn't about the team. He deserves to get caught. We worked hard on those sets, and what they did to Luke's locker definitely wasn't right."

"But Luke doesn't even want to turn the guy in," I said. "He figured out that it was Stillman too. I bet the whole school will know before long."

Jenna looked at me and shook her head. "It's not just up to Luke," she said. "You know who's responsible for this. You know what's right. It shouldn't be left up to the victim to turn Stillman in. Luke's probably worried about what Stillman would do to him if he went to the principal."

I had to agree with Jenna, as usual. Of course Luke would be worried. He was half the size of Ben Stillman. Then again, Lukas was no coward.

"Don't you think it's going to look weird if I narc on Stillman, though?" I asked. "Some people might think I'm doing it just to get him out of the way."

"Kyle," Jenna said firmly, "you've got to stop worrying so much about what other people think. You have to figure out what's the right thing to do and do it."

For the rest of that day, I thought about what Jenna had said. This whole situation had seemed so complicated. But when you broke it down the way she had done, it was simple. Do the right thing. Even if it's difficult.

I decided to do just that. As I went to sleep that night, I was already planning what I'd say to Principal Jensen and, if necessary, to Coach Williams and all my teammates.

chapter fifteen

I had basketball practice before school, so I knew I wouldn't have time to talk to the principal until lunch hour. Still, I made sure I arrived at school early. In fact, I was already dressed and shooting free throws when Ben Stillman strode through the double doors of the gym.

Judging by the sullen look on his face, this hadn't been the easiest of weeks for him. He headed for the locker room but was quickly intercepted by Coach Williams. "Stillman," the coach said. "I need to talk to you."

"After practice, Coach?" Stillman asked.

"No, right now," came the curt reply.

The rest of us stood there, basketballs on hips, staring at one another. The coach and Stillman walked into the coach's office and shut the door behind them. Coach Williams drew the shades on the window that looked into the gym. This was definitely serious.

Ten minutes later, the door opened and Ben, now ashen-faced, walked out. Not just out of the coach's office, but out of the gym as well.

Coach Williams blew his whistle. "Everybody to center," he shouted.

We all assembled at midcourt and sat in a horseshoe formation in front of Coach.

"People," he said slowly. "I've got to say, this has been an awful week for me and for Sainsbury basketball."

I looked at Sammy and shrugged my shoulders. He stared back blankly. We knew something bad was coming.

"Ben Stillman is no longer a member of our team," the coach continued. "Nobody came forward, but the police have identified him from the videotape of the theater incident. He was with Flatley and Armstrong when they wrecked those sets. And he just admitted to me now that he took part in the locker vandalism too.

"I had no choice. I had to suspend Ben and the others for the rest of this season. All three of them will be on student probation until after Christmas. They will also be required to attend awareness meetings put on by PFLAG—Parents, Families and Friends of Lesbians and Gays. The police are considering whether to press charges."

For the umpteenth time that week, my mind was reeling. Stillman was gone, along with Armstrong and Flatley. It was shocking news, but at the same time it felt like justice had been done. Then again, it brought some serious consequences for our basketball team.

"I don't have to tell you that this will obviously hurt our chances of winning the regionals," the coach continued.

Heads nodded all around.

"But you know," he added, "some things are more important than winning and even more important than basketball itself. That's a lesson we've all learned this week, I think."

These were words I had never expected to hear from Coach Wayne Williams. I had played four years for him. I had long thought basketball—and winning—were more important to the man than absolutely everything else. But I had to admire him for one thing: He wasn't babying big Ben Stillman any longer.

The fact the police had picked out Stillman from the videotape instantly made my life a little easier. I no longer had to worry about going to Mr. Jensen or about what people would think about me turning in my teammate.

In that sense, I was relieved. But it didn't change the fact that basketball at Sainsbury had been radically altered. With Ben Stillman on the team, we had been city and regional favorites. Now we would be hard-pressed to make the play-offs. And it didn't change the fact that I hadn't exactly been a good friend to Lukas. Stillman and his buddies had committed the vandalism on Luke's locker, but I was the one who had turned my back on him for years.

The guys were subdued as we ran through the remainder of practice. The mood hadn't lightened much in the locker room as we all got ready for school.

"There goes the season," said Layne Dennis, a senior in his final year of high-school basketball.

"Yeah, all because of that little faggot," added Alex Morton, another twelfth-grader.

Everybody in the locker room knew Morton was referring to Lukas. Nobody said a word. But this time, I wasn't going to sit silently by while my friend got slagged.

"Shut up, Morton," I growled. "Stillman and Flatley and Armstrong got just what they deserve. They're idiots."

The six-foot-two Morton stiffened and cast a sour look my way. "What they did was just a joke, man," he sneered. "Pukas is so sensitive, just like a dainty flower. His feelings get a little hurt and our whole season gets trashed."

I'd had enough. I rushed across the locker room toward Morton, not sure what I was going to do once I got to him. It never happened, though. Pete Freeman and Sammy Curtis intercepted me. "Chill," Sammy said. I slowly sat back down in my stall.

"Evans is right," Freeman said, eyeing Morton, a warning tone in his voice. "Shut up about Lukas Connor. None of this is his fault. He didn't do anything to anyone."

Heads nodded in agreement all around the locker room. Morton was obviously deflated. He dressed quietly and left. One by one, everybody else on the team did the same. And although we didn't talk any more about it, I somehow felt that most of us had grown up a little bit.

The mood on the team had brightened considerably by Friday as we loaded onto the bus for the ride to Echo Valley, a twenty-five-minute drive north.

Echo Valley had never been a powerhouse in our league. Their school was less than ten years old. It had been built to accommodate families who couldn't afford the soaring house prices in the city. But the Echo Valley Badgers had slowly been working their way toward respectability. This season they had their best team ever.

The Echo Valley gym was already nearly full as we entered, wearing our blue-and-gold Sainsbury jackets and the shirts and ties Coach always made us wear on game day. It felt weird to walk into an opposing gym without Ben Stillman in the lineup. Even though I didn't like the guy, I had to admit we had been a lot more intimidating when he was with us.

In the locker room, even Coach Williams seemed different. His pre-game pep talk was muted compared to his usual over-the-top message. "Look, boys, we've had a tough week," he said. "But I know you will go out there and represent your school well. Do that, and I'll be happy."

The gym was absolutely packed as we entered from our locker room, each dribbling a ball to begin our warm-up drills. The crowd was buzzing. The Echo Valley band roared through the school's fight song. But over all that noise, I still managed to hear some familiar voices from the stands just above our bench: "Go get 'em, Eagles! Kick some Badger butt!"

I spun around and caught sight of Jenna's face in the crowd. I knew she had been planning to be at the game, so her presence didn't surprise me. But the smiling faces of the kids packed around her certainly did. There beside Jenna were Lukas Connor, Ollie Jacobs, Brad Schmidt and several other members of the *Oliver!* cast.

I was blown away by the fact that these kids had all caught rides to Echo Valley just to watch us play. Others on the team noticed as well. "Sweet. A cheering section for a road game that includes somebody besides our parents." Sammy laughed as he passed me following a layup.

The presence of the Sainsbury drama group put some extra bounce in my step during the rest of the pre-game warm-up. I was as pumped as I had ever been for a game. And I would have to be jacked. Without Ben Stillman in the lineup, it was going to be tough going against Echo Valley.

The Badgers had a pair of twins—German exchange students named Dieter and Frederick Heintz—each standing six-foot-five. I had heard about these guys, but seeing them in person, I knew we were in trouble. I looked over at Sammy, my new frontcourt partner in the starting unit. I knew he was thinking the same thing. Without Ben, we were definitely outsized in this one.

Sammy took the jump, a surprise to Echo Valley since I was a couple of inches taller than him. But all of us who had played against Sammy in practice knew he had a huge vertical leap. He outjumped Frederick Heintz by a good three inches, shocking the blond-haired German. The ball went directly to Layne Dennis, who whipped it upcourt to me. I streaked to the basket for an easy layup, and we were up 2-0.

For three quarters of the game, things couldn't have gone any better for the Eagles or for me. Coach was calling my number a lot more often and, for some reason, I was really "feeling it" in this Echo Valley gym. By the end of the third, I already had twenty-five points and Sammy had fourteen. More importantly, our team led the Badgers by ten points. And we had managed to suck much of the life out of the home crowd.

"All right, guys, just one more quarter," Coach Williams said in the huddle. "Just do what you've been doing. You guys are looking great out there."

Maybe the coach's words were a jinx, but as soon as we took the court for the fourth quarter we suddenly didn't look the least bit great. Passes that we had completed routinely over the first three periods were fumbled away. My shot deserted me completely. It was only the shooting of Layne Dennis that kept Echo Valley from storming back and going well ahead.

With twenty-five seconds left in the game, and Echo Valley trailing by just two points, the Badgers worked the ball inside on the high post to Dieter Heintz. The beefy forward spun and knocked me over as he drove his shoulder directly into my chest. At the same time, he flicked the basketball desperately toward the hoop with his left hand. The ball fell through the net.

But I knew it wouldn't count. He had clearly charged me on the play.

Unfortunately, that's not the way the official saw it. His whistle blew all right, but he pumped his fist downward, signaling that the basket was good. Then he pointed at me and called me for a blocking foul. It was my fifth. I was out of the game.

Helpless, I walked slowly to the bench. The game was out of my hands now as the hulking German went to the free-throw line. Dieter calmly stepped up and nailed his foul shot. Echo Valley led by one. The home crowd was again going crazy.

Still, we had the ball and a great chance to win. Coach Williams called a time-out. We huddled around him, sweat dripping off our arms and foreheads. We were all waiting for him to call the final play.

Normally in a situation like this, the ball would go to Ben Stillman. But everybody knew that wasn't going to happen. Now that I had fouled out, there weren't many inside options left for us.

"Okay, guys, here's what we're going to do," Coach Williams said. "Everybody's going to expect it to go outside, since our regular big men are gone. But let's get it inside. Sammy, the ball is coming to you. Are you ready?"

Sammy nodded. I could tell he was nervous, but I also realized how excited he must be. And nobody on the team would have a problem with him taking the last shot. Nobody worked harder than Sammy Curtis.

Pete Freeman inbounded the ball to Layne Dennis who, as coach had instructed, dribbled the clock down to five seconds. Then he looked for Sammy, who had come to the high post after being freed on a screen. Sammy caught the pass from Dennis, pivoted and was wide open. He launched the shot from just inside the free-throw line as the buzzer sounded.

Everybody in the steamy Echo Valley gym watched the ball sail toward the rim. The arc looked good and so did the distance. On the bench, I raised my arms in triumph, only to see the basketball bounce gently off both sides of the rim and fall harmlessly to the ground. Somehow, it had managed to stay out of the basket.

The gym exploded. The Badgers jumped into each other's arms. Dieter Heintz was mobbed as Echo Valley celebrated the biggest victory in its school's short history.

We ran off the court, holding our heads high. Our once-promising season had started 0–2. We weren't the same team anymore. Every game we played now was likely to be a struggle.

Each of us knew that our chances of winning a regional title had been hugely decreased by the events that had taken place that week. But somehow, as we exited the court to cheers from Jenna, Lukas and the rest of their group, each of us also knew that Coach Williams had been right: Winning wasn't the only thing that mattered. And that was okay.

chapter sixteen

Four weeks later, I stood next to Lukas backstage in the Sainsbury theater. We peeked around the edge of the thick blue curtain. More than two hundred people had already found seats. There was still half an hour before the performance started.

"You nervous?" Luke asked.

"Nah." We both knew I was lying.

Tonight was the big night—the dress rehearsal for *Oliver!* I knew that Mom and Dad were going to be in the crowd. About four hundred people were expected to pack the theater. The cast and crew had been allowed to invite family and friends to the dress rehearsal free of charge. It would be the first time we'd perform the entire show in front of any kind of an audience. And it was my first time being on stage for something other than a regular rehearsal. Of course I was nervous.

The last month had whizzed by in a blur of basketball practices, rehearsals for *Oliver!* and schoolwork. Coach Williams and Ms. Lawson had been right: I had taken on a big load.

But even though I'd had no time to watch TV, play Xbox 360 or just hang out, I had been having a blast. I felt part of everything big that was happening at Sainsbury High. And I'd never had more friends.

After our loss to Echo Valley, we had turned things around on the court, winning three of four games against weaker teams in the conference. Basketball had become fun again, especially without Ben Stillman in the mix. We had blown our shot at the conference and regional titles with three losses already this season. But even though we weren't as strong, playing somehow felt better than it had before. Coach didn't seem so intense and stressed-out, and now we had only a single jerk—Alex Morton—in our lineup. No one hassled me anymore about being in the play, either.

Basketball wasn't on my mind tonight, though, as I stood behind the curtain with Lukas. Instead, I was hoping—praying, really—that I could make it through this performance without forgetting my lines or how to sing.

I had been nervous before basketball games, but never like this. My hands were shaking. I could barely get words out without trembling.

"Kyle, relax," Lukas said. "Everything is going to be fine."

I looked back at Luke. If he was nervous, he was doing a great job of hiding it. He was in costume as Fagin: black cape and coat, high boots and the cut-off gloves of an aging pickpocket. The makeup crew had done an amazing job of aging Lukas. It was hard to believe it was him.

I had seen more of Luke over the last six weeks than I had in the last six years. I'd come to appreciate just how hard he worked at acting and singing. He was naturally talented, sure, but he had also put in hours with Ms. Lawson, honing his English accent and making sure his mannerisms were perfect. He had managed to find time to help me rehearse too.

The more I hung out with Luke, the more I admired him. He was smart, funny and a friend you could count on. At the same time, I realized what a dork I'd been for ignoring him all these years. Worse than a dork, if I was being honest. But not anymore.

I felt Jenna's hand slip into mine as I stood waiting for the show to begin. "You'll be great," she whispered soothingly. "I'm shaking too, you know."

Seconds later, Ms. Lawson began calling out instructions. Each member of the cast and crew sprang into action. After six weeks of rehearsals, I was confident I knew where to go. But could I deliver once I got there?

The house lights dimmed. I heard a buzz roll through the crowd. The Sainsbury band began playing a shortened version of the music that would be in the show. When they got to a snippet of "Consider Yourself," I gulped. The next time I heard that music, I'd be singing—all by myself. Like a tightrope walker without a net.

The curtains finally opened. Little Jake Barnett, as Oliver, was dressed in rags and holding a huge wooden bowl. Jake was so tiny and pitiful-looking that he had the audience eating out of his hand before he said a single word. By the time he'd been chased around the stage by mean Mr. Bumble, the crowd was fully engaged.

It seemed like only seconds later that Ms. Lawson was calling our names. "Kyle, Luke," she said. "Next scene."

As the curtains closed and the stage-hands quickly put up the set for Fagin's hideout, I scurried into place with the rest of my pickpocketing gang. I would open the scene sitting on a barrel playing cards with the rest of the boys.

The curtain opened and I stared wide-eyed out at the audience. It might have been four hundred people, but it seemed like four thousand. I searched the crowd for Mom and Dad but no luck. However, one group near the front of the stage did catch my eye.

Most of the Sainsbury basketball team, including Coach Williams, was sitting together on the left side of the theater a couple of rows from the front. Sammy Curtis was carrying a cardboard sign. It read: *Break a leg, K-Man!* Coach gave me the thumbs-up and a wide smile as I stared back at the group, dumbfounded. Ever since Stillman's suspension, Coach had been more supportive of my role in the musical. It was as if he'd decided that maybe it was okay for a kid to be into other things as well as basketball. The other players, with the exception of Alex Morton, had followed his lead. Even so, I was surprised to see them in the audience, and I almost missed my cue.

"Dodger, this is Oliver. Oliver Twist," Fagin said. "I trust you'll make 'im feel at home."

It was too late for nerves now. "As you wish, Fagin," I replied as loudly as I could in my best Cockney accent. Then I waited for the orchestra.

The band began playing. There was nothing left to do but trust myself and the hours of singing practice I had put in.

"'Consider yourself, at home,'" I sang. "'Consider yourself, one of the family...'" The sound of my voice coming over the speakers hanging above the stage startled me, but at least I was on-key so far. With the first few lines of the song, my nerves eased, and I became Dodger. All the anxiety I'd felt before this performance melted away. In its place came a wild rush of excitement.

The evening had begun with me almost dreading to get up on stage. But forty minutes later, as it ended with sets of characters taking bows before a standing ovation of family and friends, I felt like I never wanted to get off the stage. The dress rehearsal had been a blast. I couldn't wait for the first show.

The crowd went wild as Jake Barnett and Jenna appeared, holding hands for their bows as Oliver and Nancy. Soon it was our turn. Luke and I trotted out, bowed to each other and then turned to the audience. The waves of applause washing over us were sweet and refreshing. Finally, I spotted Mom and Dad, standing and waving about ten rows back. Next to them were Lukas's parents.

The curtains closed and I turned to Luke. "You were awesome, man," I said, slapping him on the shoulder.

Luke looked at me, the hint of a grin forming on his face.

"You were pretty good yourself," he said with a wink. "For a jock, that is."

I grabbed Luke in a headlock and gave him a playful noogie. The past six weeks had been a little crazy, but the end result was that the two of us were back to being great friends. And I knew nothing was ever going to change that again.

Jeff Rud was a sportswriter and colum-
nist at various newspapers in Canada for
twenty years. He is now a political reporter
for the Victoria *Times Colonist* and the
author of numerous sports-related books,
including *High and Inside*, *In the Paint*
and *First and Ten*, all published by Orca.

orca sports

Visit www.orcabook.com for more Orca titles.